ALL THAT'S BEST OF WINTER LIGHT

March Madness, part 3

MARK FOGARTY

ISBN: 978-1-300-72705-7

WRITE ME IF YOU LOVE

COLLEGE WOMEN'S BASKETBALL!

markfogarty54@yahoo.com

VALLEY PRESS

PO Box 1691

Rutherford NJ 07070

For additional copies:

http://lulu.com/content/13640815

Also available from Amazon.com, Amazon Kindle and other Internet retailers

Table of Contents

ACKNOWLEDGEMENTS

"Lovers and Fighters" and "The Rebound" were written by Mark F. Fogarty. Copyright 2013 Mark F. Fogarty

I want to thank Melanie Klein for reading and commenting on these pages.

This book is respectfully dedicated to Coach Maggie Dixon, gone too soon.

ALL THAT'S BEST OF WINTER LIGHT

You Ain't Much If You Ain't Dutch

The building is on fire again. I can barely see through the smoke, which I wave away from my eyes. Then I see a small figure running at me. *Make it this time!* I think, and hold out my hand to her. She is getting closer and closer, bigger, she stretches out her hand… there is a loud *boom!* and the fireball engulfs her just before I can pull her to safety. "Daria!" I yell, reaching out wildly. The fireball never engulfs me, only her. It's as if there's a shield or divide between us, as if we are on different sides of the universe.

I look around me. I'm sitting up in bed. My wife is close to me, hesitating to touch me before I'm out of the nightmare world. When she sees I recognize her, she puts her arms around me. That's not as easy to do as it would be usually. She is eight months pregnant.

"Which dream?" Dee says.

"It was the Daria dream."

The Daria dream is the worst of them, but not the only bad one. In one, I'm torn apart by wolves. In a second one, Viet Cong are just about to catch up with me. Trauma dreams, the doctor says.

"How long will I have them, doc?" I said on my last visit. "It's been nearly two years since I couldn't save Daria from the fire at the Wreck." And here's what I love. This highly-paid specialist shrugged his shoulders. "Depends," he said.

So, it's *physician, heal thyself* for me from now on.

Dee goes back to sleep, while I wait for dawn in the chair by the foot of the bed. Dawn always cheers me up. I never get the trauma dreams during the day.

Here's the winter light, not yet the sun, creeping through the curtains. This will be a good day for me, for I have an interview with the Scorpion, the athletic director for the University of Monroe Metrics. My wife has just started her maternity leave from being the head coach of the women's basketball team, with her able assistant coach, Priscilla Barnes, filling in for her. And I have the feeling that we're going to talk about me coming back to the team, with which I have a long connection.

Once a Metric, always a Metric, I think to myself. And I am looking forward to becoming poetry coach of the team again. Basketball is the opposite of death, and I want to wrap it around me like a flag on the fourth of July. Beauty, grace, precision, high ambition, explosive force towards a repeated gratification. Every 30 seconds, a triumph or a setback. There is nothing like it in the world. Except maybe having a baby.

Not even March Madness yet! I thought to myself as I stood in front of the gymnasium door. Snow was swirling around my face, but it was the last week of January, so that wasn't unusual. The sign in front of me said TEMPORARY HOME OF THE MONROE METRICS, and the wind had blown the banner lopsided. Not very impressive. Above it, in larger scripted letters carved into the masonry, was UKVK. The University of Kill van Kull, our crosstown rivals (though they had slipped into Division II). How long had it been since I'd visited the Metrics? I couldn't remember. Not as often this year as last. But I'd been to a few games to watch Dee patrol the sidelines, shaking her head at how inept the team had suddenly become.

The team was sharing this gym space with the Killers, as it had the past year as well, because our new home arena, the Wreck, wasn't quite finished yet. It was only about three miles from the Kill Zone. I'd just driven past it on my way over. Almost finished, almost ready to move into. With a big opening game, the last of the season, against Notre Dame. *The Dames*. I laughed to myself at how the 2012 Metrics had tagged them. The Fighting Irish didn't think it was funny. Best not to rile them up, either.

I pushed open the door. There was a rent-a-cop at a desk who signed me in and told me where to go. (I hadn't been to the locker area before, just the auditorium to watch the game.) *Ugh!* There was a bad smell in this place. Not just sweat. I was used to and even enjoyed the smell of what I called virtuous sweat, ginned up by a passionate physical effort (though I preferred it to be dispelled shortly after in the showers). But this was a smell of another kind, of envy maybe, jealousy, bad blood. It had been nice of the Killers to offer to share their gym for the two seasons the new Wreck was being built. But the marriage hadn't gone smoothly.

In the visiting team's usual back-of-the-house, where the Killers had put us up, the offices were ridiculously tiny. The coach's office, where I could see the Scorpion through the glass walls, was so small it had no door!

"What a shithole!" I said to the Scorpion as I came in. He was reading something through half-glasses. Was it my imagination or had his toupee grown in the past year? There was only one chair, so I sat down in it.

"Counting the days until the Wreck opens," the Scorpion said. "State of the art facility. Beautiful. You been inside? No? I'll take you over for the nickel tour when we're done here."

"Could be a great time for a poetry coach," I said, to cut right to the chase. I'd been the poetry coach on the 2015 squad. "I'm ready to come back."

"We need more than a poetry coach," Scorpion said. He paused. "How's Dee?" he said.

"Fine," I said. "Superhealthy. Getting a little broody recently, but I guess that goes with the territory. Baby's doing fine, the docs say."

"You know," the Scorpion said, "I wish you'd do your family planning around the Metrics' schedule. April would be a better time than February for the kid to drop. Don't get me wrong, we're all happy for you and Dee. But I hate for my coach to be on the sidelines."

"Baby ready, he comes," I said. "It's good to know, though, you want her back. Some of the media and the fanny fans want her fired." I meant the intellectuals on sports radio.

"Not her fault the team is sucking so bad," the Scorpion said. "So many transfers, injuries, she doesn't have the horses, or the houses, to carry the team."

"Ha," I laughed at his joke, which referred to Horse and House, the two stars of the 2015 Metrics who had won the Beast, the Northeast regional tournament. "What's our record now anyway? I've lost track."

"We're 7-15," Scorpion said. "Could be our worst season ever, I'd have to look it up. But I want to keep Dee. I got spoiled by so many seasons with Littlejohn—that was our hall of fame coach of 39 years, retired at the end of 2015—but I also got to know what a great coach looks like. And Dee has it. Man, she did a great job last year, winning 25 games."

That team, the 2016 Metrics, had made it to the Beast finals and to the semi finals of the national tournament before losing, in both cases, to the Dames.

"Final Four first time out of the box," I agreed with him. "But look, God willing and the creeks don't rise, she'll be back next year. And Priscilla is a great coach. She'll do great until Dee comes back."

"Oh, I'd agree with you," the Scorpion said. "Except for one little fact. She gave me her resignation, not an hour ago."

"What?" I said.

"She's going to be assistant coach at Notre Dame," Scorpion said, "and with Muffet ready to retire in a year or two over there she has a clear route into the head coach's chair."

"Wow," I said. This was hard to digest. As a senior, Priscilla Barnes had scored the bucket that ended the 2013 NCAA Final in our favor, and then had come back to the squad as an AC for the 2015 team. So she was connected with the three greatest teams in the Metrics' storied history, adding in the Women of Monroe (2012) and the Wild Horses (2015). I literally couldn't perceive her as being anything other than a Metric.

"She's cleaning out her office now," the Scorpion said, "if you want to say goodbye. Although I guess we'll see her again for the opening of the Wreck. It's a great opportunity for her."

It sank in on me. "Who's going to coach the team? Al Romero?"

"No," the Scorpion said, waving his hand. "I like Al, but he isn't head coach material, even part time. I wish you'd get with him and tell him how you got off the sauce," he said. "Al is getting worse and worse."

This wasn't the right time to talk about sobriety, although I had my ideas about it for sure. "Who then?" I asked.

"I've been thinking about it for the past hour," the Scorpion said. "And here's the deal. You're right. I was going to ask you to come back as poetry coach. But you know the team, the gals like you, you know Dee's methods, and it's only temporary," the Scorpion said. He paused. "And I've always felt guilty about firing you right after we won the Beast. In short," he said, "I want you to be head coach for the rest of the year."

So Priscilla and I both had big news when I walked down to her airless cubby down the hall. She was stuffing yellow lined pads into a cardboard box. She handed me a Metrics cap, royal blue, of course.

"Guess I won't be needing this any more," she said. "Let Dee know this just came up alla sudden," Priscilla said. "I wasn't planning to go."

"You'll have to get in line," I said. "First I have to let her know what came up for *me* alla sudden."

"You'll be fine," Priscilla said. "How many thousands of basketball games did you watch as a reporter? You know how the game is played. And you really loved the Wild Horses squad, you're good with the ladies. You were good with me, when I was on the cane and thinking about the future."

Priscilla was thinking about the 2012 team, the Women of Monroe, when she'd been injured and accompanied the team walking with a cane.

"It was then I stopped playing the game and started watching it," she said. "And you helped me visualize the future. You and Eduardo."

Eduardo was the now-legendary P.C., the first poetry coach any team ever had. He'd inspired the Metrics into the NCAA Finals, and even though they lost to Constitution, that was an *and-one* season. Eduardo's reign was short, though, and it wasn't too much later that he succumbed to mental illness by killing himself. He'd been a tough act to follow when I was poetry coach of the 2015 squad, the Wild Horses.

"More Eduardo than me," I said. "They're going to have a little corner on him in the Hall of Fame room in the new Wreck."

"I'm glad to be coming to the opening of the Wreck," she said.

"Don't be too happy," I said. "We're going to kick your butts."

Priscilla laughed. "No offense," she said. "But I've seen both teams. If you were a betting man you'd take the Irish to cover a six point spread," she said.

“What do I need to know about the team?” I asked.

“Ask Dee!” Priscilla said. “Alright, alright. You remember Earlene from the 2015 squad. Junior now.”

Who could forget Earlene Manigault, the Goat? She’d only scored the winning basket in the Beast final against Constitution. She’d be a famous Metric forever, and had the potential of being one of the best players ever in the women’s game.

“Well, she’s off her game. Physically she’s fine, so it must be something emotional. We have a soph named Vanessa C. Blalock.”

“Vanessa C,” I said. Tough forward. Insisted on the initial. To the point of fisticuffs.

“They’re both from Sheridan City, local girls, so I’ve been trying to find out from her what it is that’s bothering Earlene. So far, no luck.”

“I used to be a reporter,” I said. “That’s a legal spy. I’ll see what I can nose out.”

“Could be because she’s the only Freak left,” she said. The Freaks were the four freshmen of the 2015 squad, the mainstays of last year’s great team. Two of them, True Lies and Wolfpick, had transferred out. The other, Isabella Matie, had sustained a season-ending injury in the first game. Took a lot of air out of the tires. Isabella had not only left the team, she’d gone home to St. Louis to rehab.

“You remember Sweet,” she said. “She’s our go-to senior, but we haven’t been supporting her. She’s a little gal, so she’s getting doubleteamed and bumped around the league.”

“Church Lady,” I said.

“Yeah. Amazing Graciela is still with the team. Senior. But the other Church Lady, W.A, graduated. Broadcast graduated. Penthouse transferred out, the publicity was too much for her.” Penthouse had bravely outed herself on ESPN in 2015, and that caused quite a commotion.

“What about the new jacks?” I asked.

"Ask Dee," Priscilla said. "She's still on the payroll. I've punched out."

"I'll miss you," I said. "I thought you'd be here forever."

"It's a gypsy life," Priscilla said. "You know that. New Netherlands today, Indiana tomorrow, Spokane next weekend."

"The Lady Zags," I smiled, remembering. "That's when the team caught fire."

"I'll take all that with me, Poetry Man," she said. That was my handle on the 2015 squad. "I loved it here. You of all people should know that. You love it here. So do I. The lights in the Wreck are bright, and you're coming down the stretch. You call the ladies in and they all huddle, five of them within two feet of you, looking at you with trust and totally convinced they're going to win, and you love them and they love each other and you know they're going to take it down. Outside it's winter, but inside it's all that's best of winter light."

I gave her a hug, and we held it a little longer than jocks usually do. "You have a little bit of the poet in you, Priscilla Barnes," I said. "But remember to bring your A game when you come back to the Wreck."

"It's stopped snowing," the Scorpion said, having returned from a scouting trip to the great outdoors. "Let me run you over to the Wreck. I tried to call a press conference, but nobody was going to come. It's been that kind of year…"

I was just putting away my phone. "That was Dee?" the Scorpion said. "Big surprise?"

"Can't tell," I said. "All she asked me was if I'd be home for dinner."

"Ha ha," Scorpion said, but I didn't know what was funny.

The AD prided himself on the old bomber he drove. This one was a Subaru with, it was said, 350,000 miles on it. I think that was an urban legend. I don't think it had any more than 250,000 miles on it.

Stuyvesant Landing, New Netherlands, across the Third River from Sheridan City, N.N., where the main campus of UM was, was covered in a couple of inches of white snow as we drove, and it hadn't been ruined yet. Soon enough it would be black from exhaust and other noxious substances, but for now it was quite pretty. More suburban than the big city, Stuyvesant Landing had parks and trees and a little gazebo right by the train station, which would get you into New Amsterdam if you were patient enough.

The Scorpion launched into an old wheeze. "Sheridan City is the only place where when it rains, it makes its own gravy." No doubt! Then he said, "Check out the fresh air!"

It wasn't hard to, since the Subaru's HVAC had given up long ago. But I was immune to the weather for once.

"How's the book business doing?" the Scorpion asked, simultaneously honking the horn at somebody to move so he wouldn't have to test the suspect brakes.

"Not bad," I said, though that wasn't really true. "The Littlejohn book is out in trade paper. The second basketball memoir is on Kindle and in paperback."

"I have to get that one," the Scorpion said. "What's it called again?"

"The Very Best of Day and Night," I said.

"Liked the first one," Scorpion said. "*The Very Best of Dark and Bright*. Right? What's next?"

"Talking to the Army about doing a bio of Maggie Dixon," I said. Maggie had been a young and gifted coach at West Point who had died suddenly and way too young.

"We went to the Maggie Dixon invitational last month," Scorpion said. This was a yearly do at Madison Square Garden in New Amsterdam. "Got our butts kicked. But I always liked her. Hey, but and butt. Pretty funny."

"Well, after the bios of Littlejohn and Pat Summitt, I'm starting to get a track record. Hopefully it will be steady work, though it puts a little pressure on the home life."

"This thing of ours," Scorpion said. "It's the life we've chosen. There she is!"

The Wreck, or the John Littlejohn Recreational Center, named after the retired Metrics coach, was hoving into view, if such a word sequence was possible. The air outside it was fresh and cold—basketball weather.

The Wreck was a neat, smallish building that had sharp angles all over, perhaps to correspond with the traditional sharp elbows of the Metrics squads. The Scorpion hopped up the steps two at a time, but I was more careful. Inevitably I was thinking about the last time I'd been on the steps of the Wreck.

The Scorpion knew it, too. "Come on," he said, "you might as well get it over with. Jump right into the deep end of the pool."

Easy for him to say. But the massive wooden doors were homey and kind of spectacular, announcing something great was waiting for you inside. And inside I was cheered to see they'd kept the grand staircases that took you up to the balcony. It was like walking in to Radio City Music Hall for the first time. You caught your breath at the scope and beauty of it. It promised something fine was going to happen if you walked up those faux-marble steps.

There were workmen all over everywhere, and a smell of painted wallboard and dust. "This place is going to kill me," he said. "It's a full-time job just managing the contractors while the GC has the no-work flu. That's why I need someone like you to run the team for me while I make sure we open on time. Nobody's expecting miracles. Just keep us from getting more embarrassed than we are now."

"Well, I don't know," I said. "The Metrics can be a pretty miraculous team if you give them half a chance, usually."

"Here's their chance," Scorpion said. "The coaches' offices, weight room, locker room aren't finished yet," he said. "They'll be real similar to the old ones, except the roof won't leak when it rains anymore. Let me show you the HoF, though."

The Eduardo Jonas Hall of Fame was a big, well-lighted place, with a lot of familiar faces. Too many, in fact.

"Don't go down that aisle," Scorpion advised. "Look here. We found a photo of Littlejohn with hair. Must be from the Civil War." I had fond memories of Littlejohn from his 39 years of patrolling the sidelines of the Wreck. He'd found a way to win 20 games a year, get 90% of his women degrees, and retire a happy and well-loved man. You could have a life a lot worse than Littlejohn's.

"Hey, the 2013 team," said the Scorpion. There was Priscilla in a larger-than-life photo, about to score the winning goal in the NCAA finals. She had her eyes on the prize and you could see there was no way she would miss the shot. The Metrics' only national championship in 30 years of trying ensued.

"Hard to believe she won't be here," the Scorpion said. "Breaking up that old gang of mine."

"She'll be here," I said, nodding at the picture. "Once a Metric, always a Metric."

"Here's Eduardo," the Scorpion said, as we got to the exhibit on the 2012 squad. I missed the Metrics' first poetry coach, and there he was again, in flying white hair and beard and a royal blue Metrics' tee out of the college bookstore, with a finger in the air to signify *poetry*!

"The Women of Monroe team," I said, calling them by their nickname. Eduardo had helped them catch fire and come to within a point of winning the national final. I'd covered the team that year as a reporter and had fond memories of Priscilla, Pip Pippin, Lady Dagger and their mates. No one thought there was an iota of loss in that squad, no matter what the final score said.

"The Wild Horses," Scorpion said, as we moved along. How could I forget? By chance I'd been named poetry coach for that team and went along on the Mr. Toad's Wild Ride that took us to the finals of the Northeastern Regional Tournament, the Beast. The only Beast we'd ever taken down. There was GG, or Horse, who had hoisted the team onto her broad shoulders to win. There was my wife, looking down anxiously at a clipboard. Hey, look at this! There I was, surrounded by my team, me with a rolled-up shirtsleeve to show them where I'd been branded with a horse tattoo to show my solidarity, they all laughing and pointing and staring. The Wild Horses. I'd loved them all in our short time together, and losing one of them had hurt me more than most people knew.

"Great times," I said.

"Let's go over to the Kaboose and get something to eat," the Scorpion said. "You'd better call Dee. You won't have time to be home for dinner."

"Why not?" I said.

"You're our basketball coach now," the Scorpion reminded me. He looked me over, up and down. "Do you even own a suit? Well, you can borrow my jacket for tonight."

"Tonight," I said. I was still back with the champion squads in my mind, and slow to come back to late January of 2017.

"Yeah, dude," he said. "You're starting tonight."

"Tonight?" I said. "Home or away?"

"Technically, both," the Scorpion said.

"Don't talk in riddles," I said.

"We're playing the Killers tonight at their home court. Our home court, too."

The Kaboose was a popular undergrad bar and grill just across the street from the old Wreck, and therefore caddy-cornered to the new one. It had an old bar smell I knew, of spilled beer and 2 AM frustrations. Its interior rooms were marked by theme. So the Pool Room had a cuestick over the door. The Jock Room had a dangling mobile of sports bras and jock straps (unused, I hope). But the food wasn't bad. Since I didn't drink any more, the food was all I had to measure the place by. I should get used to it, I thought I remembered from my reporter days how bad the eats were when you followed a team on the road.

"What do I need to know before I go back to the lion's den?" I asked. "Why are we sucking so bad?" I asked the Scorpion.

"We were looking for big things from the Goat," he said. "Freshman year, you saw how she did. Last year, breakout year. With two more years to play, we positioned her as the franchise star. But it hasn't worked out. Something on her mind. She's moody, she's sullen. Never know when she's going to show up for the game. Use some of that poetry thing of yours. Get inside her skull and bring the real Earlene out."

"But I'm the head coach now, not the poetry coach," I said. "Unless you've changed your mind?" Ribs arrived, and the Scorpion laughed and shook his head. "So that's a different gig."

"Yeah, but how much?" the Scorpion said. "Aren't you the same person?"

"I don't know," I said. "Never been a head coach before. I saw how Littlejohn did it. I saw how Dee did it. But as to how I'm going to do it, I don't know. Maybe we should see if there's somebody else we can build the team around. Sweet, for instance."

"Sweet's not the same since Isabella Matie got hurt," Scorpion said. "We're just not getting the ball to her. And the bigger girls are pushing her around."

"Who's the biggest gal on the team?" I said.

"That would be Starbucks or Vanessa C. Blaylock," the Scorpion said. "Vanessa C's feisty but a bit of a loose cannon. Hothead. She gets into fights with the other players. The other day I had to separate her from the Russian girl, Lara."

"She's Ukrainian, not Russian," I said. Lara was a local. There was a big community of Ukies in the Sheridan City area. They were all goodlooking people, and tall, they all seemed to be good at volleyball. Our volleyball team finished third in the country last year, behind UCLA and Pepperdine, both out in Cally where the sun shines all year round. Lara had been cut from the volleyball team for brawling, but Dee thought she could use a brawler, so she rescued her from a lost scholarship.

"Ukie, Russian, what's the difference," the Scorpion said. "She keeps her arms up in the air and blocks a few, she'll be okay for us. But don't you talk about this all the time with Dee?"

"Well come on, she doesn't want to spend her whole life talking about the team," I said. "Plus we've got a Big Event coming, so we talk about that."

"What kind of a bun do you have in the oven?" the Scorpion said.

"We're going to wait and see," I said. "In my family, we have mostly boys. Like a three-to-one ratio. But we'll take whatever comes and pray it will be healthy."

"When's the due date?" Scorpion wanted to know.

"Last week of February," I said.

"It figures," said the Scorpion. "Just when we're opening the new Wreck."

"What about morale?" I asked.

"It's tough to keep it up, losing this often," the Scorpion said.

"We need a name, like the Women of Monroe or the Wild Horses. Having a proud name gets the fires started."

"Can't help you with that," the Scorpion said. "The only nickname they have is the Raggedy Asses."

"Not going to cut it," I said. "I'll try and think of a new one."

"Good luck with that," he said.

I pointed at the Scorpion's face. "You're wearing the sauce," I said.

"Saving it for later," he said with a grin, dabbing at his face with a napkin.

"Let's pay and get over there," I said.

"Yeah, sure. Listen, if you don't mind, I'll just introduce you to the squad and then I've got to book," he said.

"Hot date?" I asked.

"I wish," he said. "It's back to the Wreck for me to make sure we're not getting gypped by the contractors."

The Tall Women's Club! But not the way I expected to see them again. Ten young women sitting on the visitors' bench in the Zone, all in the Metrics' white uniforms with the same expression on their faces, angry puzzlement. I was standing in front of them wearing the Scorpion's jacket after a very perfunctory introduction from the Scorpion, after which he'd hurried off.

The ladies were surprised. And not happy.

"Mr. Dee," one said, derisively, and I earned my first handle. "A big fat T!" another one squawked. And a third one said, "We want a coach, not a babysitter."

"Alright, listen here," I said. "Coach Johnson is my name. Some of you know me from the 2015 squad. Sweet, Goat. Amazing Graciela."

"I remember we prayed together," Amazing Graciela said.

"We haven't got a prayer this year," another one said.

"Okay," I said. "I see we got the smartass remarks to get out of the way. Anybody else have something to say?" There was some mumbling, but soon enough silence ensued.

"Okay," I said. "First, let me say my door is always open to you. That's literally true, there's no door. Let me get a look at you and see if you're as bad as everybody says." And I walked up and down the bench, slowly.

"There's a technical term for how the team's been playing," I said. "And that's PLS. Playing like shit. I'd like to change that. How about you guys?"

I stopped in front of Sweet. I had to show I wasn't going to play favorites. Sweet was only five foot six, so I could look down on her topknot. "Sweet. Why are you playing like PLS?" I asked. "You're running out there like you're carrying a piano on your back. Let's work on taking that load off."

I moved farther along the bench. "Vanessa C, stand up," I said. She had blood around her mouth and a swelling lip. "What happened to you?"

"Slipped in the shower, coach," she said, pulling her varicolored hair back around her ears.

Well, maybe. But then I saw that Lara, the big Ukie, had the beginnings of a shiner. "Lara, stand up. What happened?"

"She called me a Russian bitch," Lara said. "I'm a Ukrainian bitch." Lara had striking blue eyes and a blondish ponytail.

"She disrespected me," Vanessa C said. "Neglected to say my initial."

"I'm not a referee," I said. "I'm your coach, so listen. I can use that fighting energy, but not against our own team. The next players to fight will go home. You two can sit the first half," I said to Vanessa C and Lara. "I want you to get mad about it. And I want you to take it out on the Killers."

"Why do they call them the Killers?" came a question from the bench. "Kullers," said another, snickering voice.

“Al Romero,” I said to my assistant coach. He and I had been colleagues and drinking pals on the 2015 team. “Why don’t you take this one.”

“You know, I’ve been wondering myself,” he said.

I looked around. With Priscilla gone, the only other member of the staff was Karla, the trainer. Karla had replaced Daria, and my intention was to talk to Karla as little as I possibly could.

“Okay,” I said. “History lesson. Why is this great state of ours called New Netherlands?”

“Dutch,” Al Romero said. “Settled by the Dutch.”

“That’s right,” I said. “Stuyvesant Landing, where we are, was named after a Dutch governor. New Amsterdam got its name from the Dutch capital. Still a lot of Dutch around here. I’m partly Dutch myself. I had a Dutch grandfather, Walter ter Horst. He used to say to me, “You ain’t much if you ain’t Dutch.”

“Used to skip rope double dutch,” one of my charges said.

“Here’s the answer,” I said. “In Dutch, ‘kill’ means river. So it’s not about killing. It’s like ‘River University.’ But we all plugged in the Killers and the Kill Zone.”

“They looking to kill us tonight,” one of the wiseass chorus opined.

“We going to let them?” I asked. “I just sat down two of our players. Who wants to start the game? Show of hands.”

It took a couple of minutes, but eventually every hand went up. “Okay,” I said. “Starbucks, you raised your hand first. You’re starting. DVD, you were next. You’re starting. Also Sweet, Goat and Amazing Graciela. Gracie, you’re a senior now and you’ve got to step up.”

“Put me in, coach,” she said.

“Okay, we’re going to use Dee’s plays because I haven’t had time to make any of my own. So you’re listening for my voice. The Kullers would love to knock us off, they hate being Division II," I said. "But they're Division II. We can beat them.

"That's our goal for tonight," I said. "But let's think longterm. What do we want to accomplish?" I walked up and down the line. No one said anything.

"Okay, I'll set the goal for the rest of the regular season," I said. "We have to have a Monroe Doctrine and here it is. It's simple. Our last game of the season is against Notre Dame, to open our new house," I said. "I want us to be a winning team when the Irish come to play. I want us to have a winning record. What will that take to do? Somebody do the math."

I think I might have smelt wood burning, but my charges were doing the math. "Come on," I said. "How many games do we have to win between now and then?"

Amazing Graciela looked up. "All of them, coach."

"That's right," I said. "We're starting all over tonight. Total reset. Whoever is playing well will start. The Beeline will get plenty of playing time, because I want our D to be so tough our starters will foul out. You keep us in the game, we only need two scorers. Sweet and Goat, you're my go-to guys on the offense."

Just then I was aware that two of the Kullers were sitting a few rows up into the auditorium, listening to everything I said. They started to make goat noises, *bah-bah-bah Billy Goat!* The Goat heard the taunting and turned around, ready to jump up.

"Don't do it," I directed her. Then I spoke to the two interlopers. "You know it's an NCAA violation to spy on the other team," I said. "Rule 6, subsection B. Penalty is termination of scholarship. I don't want to see you around my team again. And oh yes, you're barking up the wrong tree making goat noises. Goat stands for Greatest Of All Time."

The two opponents didn't stick around for long. But one of them had to take a final shot. "We're going to kick your raggedy asses tonight. See how you like it in Division II."

When they left, I said, "no matter what happens in the locker room, we stick up for each other outside. That's what it means to be a team."

"Pretty good, Mr. Dee," said Starbucks. "What subsection was that again?"

"I don't know," I said. "I made it up. Okay, time to get out on the court."

It took me a little while to find Dee's playbook, and when I got back out on the floor it was almost tip time.

Here I go into the deep end, I thought. I looked around the arena. It was bright there, and that never failed to cheer me. It was about half full, and I'm guessing lot of those were Kullers fans. But some of them were our fans; it was our court too. And they were subdued. There wasn't the noise level I expected. Losing team syndrome?

No. I turned to Al Romero and said "Where the hell are the Diametrics?" It was their absence I was feeling. The band and cheer squad didn't travel to every away game, but they always came to the home games.

Al shrugged his shoulders. "They go to those band exhibitions, and sometimes they miss games. They'll be back next time." The Diametrics were one of the best-known marching bands in the country, but they would never win a drumline contest. Still, they were smartass and funny, and they could play like mofos. I needed them behind the bench if we were going to start winning.

The buzzer sounds, and it is tip time.

"What's the good word, Al?" I ask him. Al has an all-purpose word he uses on any occasion.

"Fuckem," he says. "Stupid Kullers."

"Now we can play ball," I say.

Being head coach is different than watching a game as a reporter or even as poetry coach. There is a lot to process. There are plays to call. I have to watch my players for fatigue or CNS, Cold Night Syndrome. I have to watch the refs to see what they are calling, and what they aren't calling. I have to scan the Kullers for strengths and weaknesses. Excedrin headache, coming straight up!

The Kullers come out hot. When it is 14-4, I call a timeout. When the players gather around me, I say, "Well, our offense sucks. So stop playing run and gun. Let's stay in the game with stingy D. Don't worry about foul trouble."

That is a good call. Our D keeps us from getting blown off the court. We are still having problems. Every play I call as an audible gets turned aside. Sweet keeps getting pushed around. But when we get into freethrows, Sweet is keeping us in the game, sinking every one.

Why aren't the plays working? I don't know. But there is no denying the evidence. So I stop calling them near the end of the half. Amazing Graciela backs out of the paint, takes a pass from Sweet, and drops a three. The Kullers miss at their end, and Starbucks comes flying down the court to get the last shot. Three Kullers collapse on her, and she turns and finds Amazing Graciela, standing on exactly the same spot. Another three, and we go into the exercise room down by six. My Tall Women are sitting on the weight benches, looking at me.

"Gracie, good eye," I say. "Sweet, good foul shooting. Defense, sticky D. Those are the good things. There's plenty of bad things, though. No rebounds at either end. I mean literally, zero rebounds. How is that even possible? They're taking two shots for every one we take. Our FGA is actually higher than theirs. So, we have to shoot more. DVD, Starbucks, I'm subbing in Lara and Vanessa C. I want you to focus on rebounds."

"Bout time," Vanessa C says.

Okay. What to say next? Then something comes to me. It is so clear!

"Now, on all our busted plays. I told you my door is always open. My door is always open, 24 hours a day. What does that say to you?"

A silence. Then, a light dawns in DVD's eyes.

"They stole our playbook," she says. "They came in here and piped our swaybook. Then they copied it and brought it back."

"I think you're right," I say. "But what was that? Swiped our pipebook?"

"I'm from Arkadelphia," DVD says, referring to the capital of New Netherlands. "We play Wordback there. You know, from the song: 'Take a word. Make it sing. Try it wit reverse swing.' "

Young people, I think to myself. *Young people is not my first language.*

"Okay, we're going to switch signs right now," I say. "We'll have to keep it simple. What can we use? We'll use numbers in the first half of the half. Then I'll switch to words. Sweet, you're going to win or lose this game for us. You have to shoot more. So I'm going to call "2" if I want you to take a 3. If I yell "3," I want you to go in and get fouled. Even better, go to the hoop and get an and one. Got it?"

"Three means two and two means three," Sweet says. "Yeah, I can keep that straight."

"Then we'll switch to words just when they're catching on," I say. "Now, what words can we use? I'm open to suggestions here. Something they won't understand."

"Let's use that gobbly-gook of DVD's," says Sweet. "Like our last road trip we get off the plane and she asks me, where's the khaki tanned? WTF?"

"Taxi stand," DVD elaborates.

"How's it work?" I ask DVD.

"Take the syllables and switch them up. They should make new words. If they don't, you vary it a little and make a new word. Or rhyme one word with the next. You could also say taxi stacksy."

I think about it for a minute. "Okay," I say. "As long as I can keep it straight. What kind of words should we use?"

"Food," Starbucks says. "I'm starving."

"Okay," I say. "Ham and cheese. What would that be?"

"Cham and heese," DVD says. "Or ham and cham. Cham's not a word. Ham and champ. Better."

"Ham and champ for a three," I say. "Now for a two, egg and cheese, what would that be?"

"Ease and chegg," DVD says. "So, ease and chug. Egg and chegg. Can be anything. First thing that comes into your mind."

"Oh, brave new world," I say. "Those are our new plays."

Sweet misses her first three threes, though she makes a three by going in and getting an and one. We're down by 10 again. I call time out.

"Sweet, you were making these threes in practice," I say. "Our next three plays, you're taking a three. Vanessa C and Goat, get under the boards. Lara and Graciela, get the ball to Sweet. Alright, hands together. Nine to the Wreck," I say.

Sweet drops two of her three threes.

"There we go," I say. Next time down the floor she goes to the hoop and gets a nasty shove that sends her to the floor. *And one!* We're down by four.

"Three!" I call. "Two!" Then, it's the second half of the second half and I'm pacing up and down the sidelines yelling "Egg and chegg!" and "Ham and cham!" like a loony. And the passes get smooth and crisp, the boards get banged, the shots fall. We catch the Kullers at 4 minutes left and cruise to an 8-

point victory. The ladies are rejoicing among themselves. I smell the virtuous sweat of victory on them.

"Eight to the Wreck!" I tell them. Boy howdy!

"I'm hungry!" DVD says. "What should we get to eat for our snackaround?"

"Ham and cham," says Graciela. "Egg and chegg!" says Starbucks.

"I'm going for the ache and steggs," DVD says.

"Head for the showers, ladies," I said. "Good job."

"Don't come in coach," said Starbucks. "Wouldn't want you to see any its and tass!"

When I was done shaking hands with Al Romero and Karla and slapping hands with the sulky Kullers, a voice called to me from behind our bench.

"Poetry Man!" There was somebody there, couldn't quite make her out because she had a Metrics hoodie over her face. She was also dragging a rolling travel bag behind her.

"You really the coach now?" said the voice. "Thought I must be tripping. Tried to get here for the game but the plane, you know."

The tumblers clicked in my brain and I knew who the stranger was. "Isabella Matie!" I said. "What are you doing here? You're out for the year."

"Guess I'm a quick healer," Isabella said. "Got my cert from the doc and I called the AD and left him a message. You do want me back, don't you?"

I got my cell out to call the Scorpion. "I'll get you activated tomorrow. You can come to practice the day after. I'm glad to see you!"

"Me too, Poetry Man," she said. "I mean, Coach."

That was me! It was starting to sink in. I was a head coach for a Division I women's basketball squad. I'd won my first game. I'd even started to speak a new language, Wordback. "Well I'll be a bun of a stitch," I said.

Taking One for the Team

The wolves aren't far behind me. I can hear them coming. It is winter and I am floundering through the snow, looking back. It is cold, and the air burns my lungs with every breath. Why not just give up? They will catch me as they had before and rip me to shreds. If I am lucky I won't feel much of it.

No, I won't wait for the pack. I struggle on through the snow to the top of a little rise. There before me is a building. If only I can get there ahead of the wolves? But now they are on me, hitting me with their hard muzzles and knocking me over. There are five or six of them. I can hear their horrible growling as they sink their teeth into me through my clothes. Then in front of me the alpha male, scowling with hatred and counting coup on me face to face. The wolf comes in close to my face. Then I feel him licking me messily on the mouth.

I woke up then, and there was my dog, Spotter, in front of me, waking me up with her slobbery kisses. Dee had already gotten up. I took a moment to compose myself.

"Nice to see you, girl," I said, and tousled her mutt-mix fur. "You don't even know."

I looked at the alarm clock on the night table. Better get a move on. I had a lot to do at the office, or at least I thought I might have, before the players came in for practice. So I showered and shaved in a hurry and clunked downstairs. There was Dee and her bowling ball, still in her bathrobe, perched as comfortably as she could get on our couch. She had a cup of decaf tea next to her; she was real careful what she put in her system while pregnant.

“Come and sit by me, baby,” she said, patting the cushion next to her.

“I’ve got a million things to do,” I said. “I should get in.”

“They can spare you for an hour,” she said. She had that calm, Zen look she’d get sometimes, at peace with the universe, collaborating with the universe. “Put this CD in for me, would you? Save me a trip.”

So I queued up her CD and sat down next to her. It was Enya. Not in Dee’s repertoire usually; I’d bought it for cultural reasons. (I’m part Irish, from my mom.) Maybe it was like a food craving or something.

“Pretty music,” she said. “I want our child to see and hear beautiful things. Shield him from the cruelty of the world as long as we can.”

“I’m with you,” I said. “Have you thought about a name?”

“Not important yet.” Dee said. “Tell you what. You suggest the name. I get right of first refusal, though.”

“Okay…Did I tell you Isabella is back?” I asked her, but she waved her hand to indicate no Metrics business this frigid morning.

So we sat in silence, holding hands, listening to the news from Orinoco, wherever that was (I hoped they weren’t on the schedule to play). It was sweet.

When the music was over, Dee turned to me and said, “Will you be home for dinner?”

“Should be,” I said. “No game today. Home by six.” Famous last words.

My first order of business was to stop in front of the F-ARTS building (Fine Arts) on the Stuyvesant Landing campus. I walked firmly through the scrunching snow and up the spiffy stairs. Inside there was a sign of how big the Diametrics had blown up to be. They had a factotum at a desk in front of their Romper Room.

"Do you have an appointment with Diametrics LLC?" the factotum asked me. He was none too friendly.

"Stuff the LLC," I said, going around the desk. "I'll take whoever is in charge."

"Can't go in there," the factotum said.

"Try to stop me," I said.

The Romper Room had a sort of virtuous smell of loud music and bad-on-purpose marching around. Unlike other times I visited the band room there wasn't the smell of marijuana. Let's hope the teaheads hadn't stepped up to the harder stuff.

"Poetry Man!" a familiar voice said to me. It was Stan. During the 2012 season I befriended him and wrote a story about the Diametrics that got them noticed by *SI*. By my calculation he must be on at least his sixth year at the school. Slow learner! Not much changed in all those years except for that little beard, the kind we'd called a *womb broom* back in the nabe. Beyond him was his compadre, Henry. Henry was lying across a couch, sound asleep. I'd never noticed before, but he had kind of a big ass.

"Don't wake him up," said Stan. "We got in about four from Cincinnati. I gave the squad the day off."

"When are you two *schmeckles* ever going to graduate?" I asked.

"Oh, we did graduate," Stan said. "Last year. And we made the Diametrics into a business. I'm the CEO and Henry is the music director, so less old-fart music from the 20th Century. We can even make it balance on the dollars if we go to enough drumline exhibitions and perform. But hey, enough about me. What about you? I heard you've been named head coach of the team. Dag nasty."

"It's true," I said. "And in my first game I turn around for support and—no Diametrics. I don't like that. I know you can't go to every away game…"

Stan interrupted, "But we can, now!"

",,,but I expect you to be at every home game."

"Don't get in a twist," Stan said. He consulted a little black book. "You're playing in two nights, right? Got you penciled in right there."

"Can't wait," I said. "Now do me a favor. Pencil yourselves in to our next nine games. You were a big part of the success of the Women of Monroe and the Wild Horses, and I want you to be the same for us."

"Well, it's nice to be wanted," Stan said. He sounded unconvinced.

"I need your help with a theme song," I said. "P.C. came up with "Women of Monroe," but you came up with "Wild Horses." I need something, and I need it quick. Whatcha got?"

"We already gave them a handle," Stan said. "The Raggedy Asses. You ever see them on a flight? They tear holes in their clothes for fun. That Starbucks, she wears different brand shoes on each of her feet. More comfortable, she says. So we give 'em a cheer. *She's got sass, she's got class, She's a real Raggedy Ass*."

"Let's retire that one," I said. "I want something new by next game against the Paycocks."

"Let me work on it," Stan said. "Maybe Henry will have an idea."

"Alright," I said. "You guys win?"

"No," said Stan. "How about you? You guys win?"

"We did. We slapped the Kullers in their own gym."

"Good for you," Stan said. "Good to have you back, Poetry Man."

"Call me Coach now," I said.

"What the hell are Paycocks anyway?" he asked. "Sounds like an escort service."

"Variation of Peacocks," I said. "Supposed to make us think they're old school, I guess.

"The Philly Paycocks," Stan tried it on for size. *"Pfui!"*

I got back in my car and somehow my radio presets had gotten scrambled. I wasn't listening to my usual station. I reached out to change the station but then stopped. What a cranking beat there was on this song! Couldn't make out the lyrics either. Maybe, maybe it was called "Some Thing." But the ride over to the KVKU gym was short and the DJ hadn't gotten back on the air yet to give the set list, so it would have to be a mystery.

Back in the Zone the players were starting to straggle in. They were supposed to go to classes in the morning, but some of them worked out in the exercise room for hours. When I came in, DVD, Starbucks, and Amazing Graciela were standing in a semicircle staring at Isabella Matie as if she might vanish as quickly as she came. They were wearing Metrics shorts and tees and were very tall.

Isabella had her shirt off but her sports bra on, so I figured it was all good. Jocks weren't very modest in general anyway. She had her bad arm up in the air. It was being rotated gently by the trainer, Karla. She was wearing a hat like Priscilla's over her bushy hair. Never mind the doctor. If Karla told me Isabella was good to go, I'd go by that.

"What do we got, K?" I asked.

"Good range of motion," Karla said. "Can hardly see the scar where she was cut. A little tenderness, but we can take care of that with Advil and hot stuff."

"She likely to re-injure it if we play her?" I asked.

"Always a chance," Karla said. "But a small chance, I think."

"Let me see you bench press something, Isabella," I said. "Doesn't have to be heavy. You've been keeping in shape, I see."

Isabella loaded up a barbell with some light weights and then lay on the bench. I stood above it to spot her. I also wanted to look at her for evidence of discomfort. But Isabella slowly but confidently pushed the bar up ten times.

"Okay," I said. "A couple of days to knock the rust off of you, and we'll see if you can still play."

As the rest of the ladies trickled in with their huge gym bags, I began to take Stan's point about them being raggedy asses. Their sweats were old and stained, their practice tees ripped and cut off above the shoulder. I thought about instituting a dress code. Then I decided against it.

"Keep your eye on Isabella for me, Al," I said to Al Romero. Al took the ladies through warmups and a few conditioning exercises. Then he wanted to run them through some plays.

"What are we calling them now, coach?" Al said to me. "Is a 2 a 3, or is a 3 a 2?"

"DVD," I called out. "We need a name for this slant and roll. What do we call it?"

"Rant and soul," she said.

"What about a pick and three?" (meaning to end up taking a three).

"Prick and tee," she said, and her teammates tittered.

"Okay, Al," I said. "Drill them on the rant and soul and the prick and tee."

Al could work up a virtuous sweat on the women when the mood took him, and he did that this time. The Beeline played the A-Team as defenders and rattled a few cages. That was good, as long as no one got hurt. The sound of basketballs banging against the floor and rim was soothing to me, and I could even stand the infernal squeak of running shoes. Shunning rues.

Al had moved over to foul shots when he came back to me. "Something not right with our gal," said Al. "She looks good, like a banana with a big yellow peel. But are we going to see all the bruises if we take off the peel?"

"Well put, Al," I said. "Tell her I want to see her."

"Yeah coach?" Isabella was in front of me in a minute.

"Come into my office," I said, patting a spot on the bench. She sat down.

"You're favoring the other arm," I said. "Dribbling with it, too. How'd you fool the doctor?"

"I can dribble, pass and shoot with either hand," Isabella said. "And I'm half a tick faster down the floor than I was before. I can do a job for you, coach."

"How many rebounds are you going to get?" I said.

"Never was a big part of my game, coach," she said. "Let the Tall Women have them."

"You can't lift your arm above your shoulder, can you?" I asked.

"Sure I can," she said, demonstrating. Then she put it down again. "Just not for very long."

"I give you props for what you're doing," I said. "You want to play and I like that."

"I love basketball," Isabella said. "I think about it all the time. I run plays in my head during classes. It's all I want to do."

"Well, we have something in common," I said. "I love basketball too. You can suit up with us, but you're not going to play until Saturday."

"I'm ready now," she said, and zipped back to the practice.

We practiced for two hours, and then I called it an afternoon. The gals hit the showers and I went into my office. I switched on the computer. Amazing how many e-mails people had sent me. I strained my thumb deleting them.

Then I remembered the insult. Ripped off on the plays! I was pissed. I took out a post-it and attached it to the drawer where the playbook used to be kept. *FUCK YOU!* I wrote on it with a Sharpie.

Al Romero skipped out at once but Karla stuck her head into my cube. “Coach, you want me to work with Isabella?”

“No,” I said. “Let’s give her some rest. I’ll give her some minutes Saturday in Rochester and we’ll see how she does. See you tomorrow.”

“Okay,” she said, and shortly afterward switched off her light and left.

The players were coming out now in ones and twos. “Goodnight, Mr. Dee!” somebody said.

“We could use a little D around here,” I aimed back.

The last one out was Vanessa C. She paused at my door.

“Coach, got a unit? Mind if I sit down.”

“No,” I said. I was pleased a player wanted to talk to me.

I was pleased too soon. “The Goat said to go along and she’d catch me up in a minute,” Vanessa C. “Mind if I wait here?”

“No problem,” I said. I decided to go fishing.

“I told her moms I’d bring her home today,” Vanessa C said. “Her moms and my moms, they’re best friends.”

“That’s great,” I said. “Listen, Vanessa C, is there something on her mind? She’s not the same gal I used to know.”

“Her mind isn’t being put to any good use,” Vanessa C said. “That’s all I’m going to say. Where is that girl, anyway?” She got up and walked back down the corridor to the locker room.

I was just getting back to the e-mails when I heard a shout. I got up and trotted down to the locker room. There I saw a bloodcurdling sight.

Vanessa C was slapping the Goat's face and shaking her. The Goat was curled up against the wall where it met the lockers. She was nude except for one sneaker, and a line of blood was running down her thigh. The other sneaker (red, I had time to note), was just a foot or two away. A syringe had been plunged into the rubber toe. *What the fuck.*

"Call 911," I said. I had the Scorpion's jacket on—I'd meant to return it to him at the Wreck—and I took it off and draped it around Earlene. She was mumbling something I couldn't make out.

"What's in the syringe?" I asked Vanessa C. "Steroids?"

"Not even, coach," Vanessa said. "Wango tango, I'm guessing."

"What's wango tango?" I said. I'd never heard of it.

"Nothing good," she said. "It's fucked up."

Earlene was semi-conscious when they loaded her into the ambulance. It was a university ambulance so there was a chance this might not blow wide. I hopped in after her.

"We got it, coach," said one of the paramedics.

"I'm coming," I said.

At the hospital I said I was her guardian (that was true just then) and they bustled her off and let me sit in an empty waiting room inside the double doors. In a few minutes the door banged open and it was Vanessa C.

"Heard nothing yet," I said. Vanessa C sat down.

"You knew about this?" I asked her.

Vanessa C shook her head. "Suspicions," she said.

We waited a couple of minutes more and then I called the Scorpion.

"Nice game," he said over the phone. "Meant to tell ya."

"We've got a problem," I said.

When I was through a chastened Scorpion said, "I'll get on the phone tomorrow and find a rehab for her. We'll decide what to do when she's out of the woods."

"I'll stay and make sure she's okay," I said.

"Thanks," said the Scorpion.

Oh shit. For the second straight night I had to call my pregnant wife and tell her I wouldn't be home for dinner. She wasn't happy.

Vanessa C decided to stay and keep me company. But I guess we both were dozing an hour or two later when a door opened with a bang and something blurry whipped by. Vanessa C figured it out before I did.

"Goat's bolting," she said. "Come on!"

I followed her, trying to keep up. I don't know how it happened but we got out through the ambulance bay. Vanessa C's car was not far away.

"Where is she going?" I asked.

"If she has got anything valuable she'll pawn it for a fix," Vanessa C said. "Let's try the Balls Hang Low. It's across the river in Sheridan City."

Vanessa C expertly glided her car across the bridge over the Third River and into Sheridan City. We got stuck in traffic so it took us an anxious time to get to the pawn broker's (not actually named the Balls Hang Low, that must have been a joke).

"Wait here," she said. "It'll be quicker."

Vanessa C was out again in just a couple of minutes.

"No way no how they seen her," she said.

"What else can we try?" I asked.

"She may try to get money from her moms," Vanessa C said.

"Where does she live?" I wanted to know.

"In the Stews," Vanessa C said.

The Stews! I thought they'd been dynamited long ago. Ugly highrise redbrick hellholes, poster child for the wrong way to house people. Stuyvesant Town, the project was actually called. But The Stews fit it perfectly.

I have to admit I was daunted for a second at the prospect of going to the Stews that winter night. But not for long.

"Let's go," I said. Vanessa C started the car.

"Not many live there now," she said. "Just a couple on each floor until they get all the evictions done. But the gangs use them for business. She can cop right in the building."

The neighborhood thinned out as we drove and became a kind of DMZ. There was something supposed to stand as a park, but all the streetlights had been smashed. Then the sign. *"Stuyvesant Town. Life Without Fear."*

I had a little fear working when we approached the first building. Vanessa C didn't even bother with the parking lot but drove up on the curb and as close as she could get to the front door. Inside, only the battery-powered light worked. No one in the lobby. Was that good or bad? It was so dim I couldn't make out any of the tags sprayed on the wall. Well, I could make out the numbers. But not the letters.

"Forget the elevators. Walkup," Vanessa C said, and I followed her as she moved toward the staircase. There was a stink in the place that I couldn't make out. But when we walked out onto the third floor it was strong again and I recognized it. Rotting garbage. The disposal was open and trash had been jammed in it until it spilled onto the floor.

"Come on," said Vanessa C. Earlene's mother's door was open and her mother was inside sobbing.

"This is the coach," Vanessa C introduced me. "Poetry Man."

“Poetry Man?” Earlene’s mother looked at me. She obviously recognized the name.

“How long ago did she leave?” Vanessa C asked. “How long?”

“Five minutes, maybe ten,” Earlene’s mother said. She had prayer beads in her hands and was working them.

“You alright, Mrs. Manigault?” I asked. She grabbed my arm. “Help my daughter,” she implored.

“Yes, m’am,” I said.

“We go up,” Vanessa C said. So it was back to the stairway. When we got to the fourth floor, she opened the door and carefully looked down the corridor.

“Peace and love,” she said to somebody who must have been there. Then she shut the door and looked at me. She shook her head. We climbed to the fifth floor.

This time I followed Vanessa C out into the corridor. The garbage smell was strong and I had time to note the garbage chute was jammed full on this floor too and to wonder how many floors the garbage mound went up until something pinged behind me and I heard a loud sound. Gunfire.

“Down!” said Vanessa C, and yanked at my arm so I’d hit the deck. There were several more bangs and a scream. I recognized the voice. It was Earlene.

Something made me get up and run to her voice. I heard one more *bang* and then the sound of running feet.

Earlene was screaming. She’d been shot somewhere, I couldn’t tell. Blood spattered on the wall behind her. Vanessa C came up behind me.

“Call 911,” I said for the second time that day.

“Nuh,” said Vanessa C. “They won’t come down here for half an hour. We got to get her to the hospital.” Before I could do anything Vanessa C scooped up Earlene into her strong arms and headed back for the stairs.

Luckily we didn’t run into anybody on the way. Vanessa C put Earlene into the back seat and I got in with her.

Vanessa C. hopped into the front and soon we crunched away from the Stews at speed.

At the hospital they told us Earlene had been shot once in the leg. She'd lost a lot of blood—it was all over me and Vanessa C.'s car—but she would probably make it.

"Good," I said. "But let me sit down a minute. I feel a little fainty."

"You'd better let me take a look at you, coach," the doctor said.

"That's all Earlene's blood," I said. "She bled on me in the car."

"Right, right," he said. "Oops. Some of it's yours," he said. "Nicked you right above the tattoo. Not serious, but let's get you bandaged up. What kind of tattoo is that?"

"Wild horses," I said. "You know, I think I'm going to heave."

That night, for once, I had no trauma dreams. And why should I? The day had been horrific enough. And it ended with me being discovered by Dee bundling my bloodied clothes into a bag for disposal so as not to upset my pregnant wife. As you might imagine, I had a lot of 'splaining to do with that one.

"Dee, if it was you the coach, and not pregnant, what would you have done? The same thing, I'm guessing."

"But I am pregnant, so I wouldn't have. And your wife is pregnant, and not interested in raising a baby alone, and why didn't you think of that first?" She was leaning against the washing machine to support her weight.

I thought about it then. She was right. I was a decent husband, but with an unfortunate trait of sometimes acting like an idiot.

"I'm sorry," I said. "I was wrong. Next time there's an incident I'll call the campus police. And if anybody from our side has to be involved, I'll call the Scorpion."

Dee looked at me very seriously. "I'm going to ask you a very important question. Listen up." She shifted her weight. "Will you be home for dinner tonight?"

This was the important question? Well, wait a minute. This was a question in code, and I'd better get it right.

"What time do you want me?" I asked.

"Six o'clock," she said.

"Six it is," I said. "You know tomorrow we're going away to Philadelphia, right? It's not even overnight, we'll bus on back. But I won't be home for dinner tomorrow night. I'm planning to pluck out a few tailfeathers on those Paycocks."

"Paycocks," Dee said. "What a stupid name for a sports team."

You think I disagreed? If you did, you've never been married.

So I was sleeping in that morning. I thought I deserved it. Spotter kept running in and out of the room, puzzled why I wasn't getting up. I was about to get up to walk her when the phone rang. It was Mookie, my agent.

"Zup?" Mookie started.

Actually, I could tell him about a couple of interesting things that were up, for once. But I was too weary.

"Samo," I said. "You?"

"Samo samo," Mookie said. "Publishers are heading for the hills, e-books are everything, and nobody's making money."

"Yuh," I said.

"So listen," he said. "I ran your proposal up the flagpole to see who would salute it. But I couldn't find any patriots."

I'd suggested to Mookie that we combine my two basketball memoirs, *The Very Best of Dark and Bright* and *The Very Best of Day and Night*, into one book, to be called *Boy Howdy!* after one of Eduardo's expressions. Both books had been kept purposely small because that was supposed to appeal to the Kindle crowd.

"Just not enough sales to justify it, they think," Mookie said. "Sorry, *bubelah.* Thought I should let you know. *I* thought they were good. Those Dimeetreks, they were very funny."

"Yeah, they're funny guys," I said. "Getting a little too big for their britches, though."

After Mookie hung up I didn't feel any more like getting up and facing the world. My career as a writer, post reporting, hadn't set the world on fire. I had the two books on the coaches, Pat Summitt and Littlejohn, and the two basketball memoirs. The coach books had done well in the women's basketball world, but that was a fairly small pond. Looked as if there was no call for that third memoir! Should stick to the coach bios. Lord knows, there were enough coaches to keep me busy! And good thing Dee had a real job, because the book money was small and intermittent.

I was getting paid for being the head coach, but also not much. I'd gotten my contract the day before. It was piece work, $1,000 a game. So, if I didn't get canned, that was $10,000 at least and at most, $21,000. Peanuts compared to what Dee earned as head coach. Basically I was a kept man.

Spotter wandered in again and looked at me with her empathetic eyes. She worried about me, I could tell. She was smart, and an excellent judge of character.

"Let's go for a walk, girl," I said. I was thinking we could both use it.

I give the AD credit. The Scorpion really earned his money on this one. He spun the story to the media that Earlene was visiting her mom and accidentally got caught in a gang crossfire. He withheld the drug part and so did the university hospital. He arranged to have Earlene transferred into a sports and drug rehab. And, he got Earlene's mother out of The Stews and into a more decent place to live. And the Stews got detonated a few months later, good riddance.

"She really going to be okay?" I asked him that afternoon in my doorless office. " 'Cause everyone told me that about Daria." Daria had lasted a month in the burn hospital before succumbing to an infection. I didn't want to lose another one.

"She'll be fine," Scorpion said. "The real challenge is when she gets out. Will she stay straight? Will she slip back? Do we take her back? Well, I'll think about that tomorrow, as Scarlett O'Hara would say."

"How did that turn out for her?" I asked.

"How about you?" Scorpion said. "How's the arm?"

"Stings a little, not much," I said.

"Well, you're a good man to have around in a crisis," he said. "Sorry I can't come to the game in Philly. The Wreck, you know."

Vanessa C. wandered in. Three people filled that little office.

"Hey AD," she said to Scorpion.

"How you holding up, Vanessa?" he asked, then quickly corrected himself "Vanessa C."

"Rough night, AD," she said. "That's why it's good the sun comes up again. We get a new 30 to work with."

"Good point," he said.

"Coach," she said to me. "The women want to see you. I'll take you back if you have a minute. We're all dressed."

"Go," said the Scorpion. "We're done here."

A team meeting! There was one every season. The Women of Monroe called in Eduardo to tell him they were dedicating the championship game to his daughter. And they'd called me in, the Wild Horses squad, to support me putting Penthouse on national TV to tell the world she was gay.

There they all were, in front of me. Looking serious, even somber. I didn't like the silence so I spoke.

"Most teams have a captain," I said. "A leader. We haven't got one. I think we should have one. Every team of our caliber has one. And let me remind you, the Monroe Metrics are one of the premier franchises in the history of women's basketball. So, whoever speaks to me, she will be our captain."

Another silence. Then Sweet spoke.

"What happened with the Goat?" she asked. "Vanessa C. clammed up on us."

I decided to level with them. "This doesn't leave this locker room," I said. "I was a reporter, I know what goes on between players and reporters. This time, you refer them to the AD for comment. Okay?"

"That's fair," Sweet spoke.

"Earlene was shot while buying drugs," I said. "She has a drug problem. She's going to be okay. She'll be spending a month or so in rehab. I hope the cure takes."

"K," Sweet said, breathing out. "The squad wants you to know, coach, that they appreciate the fact that you'd take a bullet for the team."

And the ladies lined up, as if it was the end of the game. And as they walked past me, each of them slapped hands with me.

DVD and Isabella were the final two to go past. I told Isabella, "We're twinsies now. I can't hold my arm above my shoulder either."

DVD slapped my hand so hard it stung.

"Gay to woe, coach," she said.

Gay to woe? Ah, Wordback. Way to go.

"What play are we running, Coach?" I said to Al. He had the women going at top speed on the floor of the Zone.

"Rum and gum," he said.

"Rum and gum. Good," I said. "Keep up the pace."

I sat down on the bench, trying to think of what other ways I could knit these players together as a team. Suddenly there was a loud *squawk* from the PA. I looked up and saw the A/V guy in the booth. He must have been testing his rig. Then I saw who the A/V guy was. It was Brad, my old buddy from the Wreck A/V!

"Back in a minute," I said to Al. I hustled to the top of the arena and then walked around the corridor until I found the A/V booth.

"Brad!" I said when I got in. "Found yourself a little extra work, I see."

"You too, coach, eh?" he said to me. I nodded.

"Listen, you know every song there is," I said. "I need your help. I heard a song on the radio yesterday but I don't know who it's by and I don't know what it's called."

"Narrow it down for me, why don't ya," he said.

"It's something like "Something," I said.

"The old Beatles tune?" he said.

"No, this century," I said.

He thought a moment. "Not coming to me," he said.

"It had some wildass rap beat," I said. "Here, let me see if I can do it for you." And I reproduced the beat as well as I could by thumping on the top of his chair.

"That's not new, coach," he said. "Sounds like an old go go beat from DC back in Grandpa's day. Pretty funky, though." He stopped and the light bulb went on. "Something. It's '1 Thing'! By Amerie. Sure, she's from DC, she would know the old go go beat."

"Can you get it over the PA?" I asked.

"Does a chef go to Asshole School? Give me two minutes and I'll get it from i-Tunes."

"Watch for my cue," I said to him.

I went back down to the floor and stopped the drill.

"Alright," I said. "We want to get that special Metrics vibe going with our team, right? So the championship teams had team handles and theme songs. That's how it works in this thing of ours. Special name, special team. Raggedy Asses is a joke. So I heard a song yesterday made me think of you all. You'll be happy to know it's from this century, not the last. Maestro!"

I cued Brad, and soon the Amerie song was booming throughout the empty (but for us) house. It got an unexpected reaction.

"That's go go!" said Al Romero. "I'm from DC." And Al started jogging up and down to the chopped-up rhythm, really getting into it until all the women were laughing and falling out. Then they got in place around him as if at a predetermined cue and started bouncing and thrusting their hips.

It was a happy rhythm and my people were linking into it and flying like you would a hang glider or something. I couldn't dance at all but I knew what the scat vocals were so when they came around the last time I sang out "Na-Na-Na-Na-Na-No! Na-Na-Na-Na-Na-No!" And the women fell out of their magic circle, laughing at me this time.

The lights were bright in the gym. Winter was at bay, for now. The winter light was sweet. We all felt the same way. We were a team.

Sweet came forward, her first decision as team captain.

"We'll take it, coach," she said. "We the 1 Things."

"Great," I said. "We know one thing nobody else knows, see."

"What that?" said Amazing Graciela.

"I'll let you know when I figure it out, Gracie," I said. "Let's get the drill done now. I have a hot date I can't afford to break."

Counting the Cars on the New Jersey Turnpike

The next morning when I went into work, I had an e-mail with the team's itinerary on it. Underneath was a bland note, "all plane charters cancelled. Chartered buses will be provided."

We don't get no respect! I remembered flying to Spokane with the Women of Monroe and flying separately to see them play in Denver. No bus trips there. Philly was only two hours away, through Jersey on the New Jersey Turnpike, so the bus made the most sense anyway. But our weekend game was to Rochester, to play the University of Kodak Shutters. That was like a 10-hour bus trip! And we were playing Providence away as well. That was a fur piece. And BC. Boston wasn't very close either.

Well, it wouldn't do to blow a gasket over it. We'd have to change their minds about where to put their resources. I decided to act out instead.

Dee was surprised and I think happy to see me coming in with a rack of ribs and macaroni and cheese. I had convinced myself she got cravings for this during pregnancy and it may be so. But I know I got food cravings during her pregnancy and this was one of them.

Spotter was happy to see me. That dog was just plain happy with everything. Too bad she'd have to wait and see if anything was left over. Dogs aren't patient. One of their few character flaws.

"What's the occasion?" Dee said.

“Can’t have dinner with my wife, we’ll be away in Philly-delphi-dilly,” I said. “So I decided to make it lunch instead.”

“How is Earlene?” Dee said. “Never saw it coming. Just knew something was wrong.”

“The GSW is no big deal,” I said. “But Scorpion told me she’s cross-addicted. In addition to the lotus she also took fetties, meth, to bring her up back to normal,” I said. “The brain damage duo. It will be a struggle for her life.”

“She’s strong,” Dee said. “She can bench press Starbucks.”

“You mean, as much weight as Starbucks can press?”

“No, she can press Starbucks above her. Good party trick.”

“Ah,” I said, bustling the plates and knives and forks. Good ribs didn’t need a fork, they fell right off the bone. Well, the check-her-tony and me’s (now I was doing the Wordback) could use a fork.

“You probably saved her life,” Dee said.

“No, Vanessa C should get the credit for that,” I said. “I was really just along for the ride.”

“Sit still, I’m paying you a compliment,” she said. “Really, why did you come home? You’re so gung ho about the team. Which is the way it should be, by the way.”

“Well,” I said, “I thought to myself *it isn’t March Madness yet*, so why act crazy? And I love to watch you sit with that faraway pregnant look, that all-powerful creating thing you have going in your belly and you stretch it out to include the whole wide world.”

“Don’t you want to make the world right for your child?” she wanted to know.

“Sure,” I said, but going into movie talk for a second I said, “But I have no such powers.” Didn’t turn out well for the Godfather either, did it? Coughed a few times (never cough in the movies, or pick up a ringing telephone, bad things will happen), keeled over in his garden, now he's pushing up the daisies. Oh well! That thing of his was totally different than this thing of ours, anyway.

"But Dee, I love to look at you. And I can't do that at work. We should get Skype!"

She looked at me for a moment. "Is that your way of telling me I'm beautiful?"

I retreated into Wordback. "You're scam dippy," I said.

She thought a moment. "War yell-come," she said. "What else was in the package?"

"Almost forgot," I said. "Got us a little something. Call it an early Valentine."

Dee took the package and looked at it with that oceanic, unfathomable look of hers. "Well, I feel special," she said. "I'll bet I'm the only girl in America to get a Checkers set for Valentine's Day."

"And before I go back I'm going to kick your pregnant butt in checkers," I said. It was way late in the pregnancy, when afternoon affection couldn't be easily expressed in other ways. Trouble is, I didn't win. Dee kicked my butt, the first of a long winning streak for her.

I was going to sit in the back with the ladies, but Al Romero knew the protocol. "This is your seat, coach," he said, pointing to the front seat next to the driver.

"Oh, er, yeah," I said. The team was making a racket in the back. Well, at least they were in good spirits.

"New Netherlands, goodbye," Al declaimed grandly as we started off on a low, cloudy afternoon from the Zone. It was obviously a motif of his. "We hope to return one day to our native land, the first state to ratify the Constitution," he said. "Oh, when!" he looked at his watch, then dropped the eloquence to say in his normal voice, "about 11 tonight, I hope."

"Al, you're a pistol," the driver said. To me, he said, "He won't sit next to you unless you ask him to. Protocol."

"Ah," I said. "Al, whyn't you join me."

"Don't mind if I do," he said.

"Any words of advice for me for tonight's game?" I had an idea of what was coming.

"Fuck'em!" he said.

From the back came a squall of complaining female voices.

"Coach, the bathroom smells like shit."

"This a real roach coach, Coach!"

"Where the movies at?"

"Settle in, Metrics," I said. "Enough of the mitch and bone. If we get to Philly in time I'll have a surprise for you."

Al was talky at first but then dozed off. Many of the players dozed off as well. I was wide awake. So was the driver, luckily. I could see the beautiful Dutch Colonials that were all over everywhere off the side of the road, most new ones but some dating back all the way to Dutch times. Big stone square things, beautiful really. *You ain't much if you ain't Dutch!*

We got to the MLK Bridge to go to Jersey (not that far, New Netherlands is just a tad bigger than Delaware, making us 49th out of the 52 states in size) and the connector to the Turnpike. The winter light was bleaching out of the sky and you had to keep your own hopes up, nature wasn't going to help you out on this day. At least there was no precip! This far south in Jersey the Turnpike was hemmed in by solid rows of trees. What was behind them? Dairy farm? Tomatoes? Super WalMart? Some mysteries are better not knowing. Very few cars too, no rush hour here. One…two…three… and we had gone two miles.

We started seeing signs of life on the approaches to the Whitewall Bridge over to Philly. Rush hour cars. In our way! The nerve! But we bulled into the city and I looked at Al's watch. Just enough time.

"Why we stopping, coach?" said a sleepy voice behind me.

"You ladies hungry?" I asked.

"We always hungry," the voice said, and I think that was true.

"You are in luck!" I said. "We have stopped across the street from Pat's Cheese Steaks, the best Philly cheesesteaks in the world. Since you ladies are hungry I'm going to treat you each to a doublewide. Here's the protocol on ordering. You order with, or without. 'Cheese steak with.' 'Cheese steak without.' Like that."

"With or without what?" said the voice.

"Onions," I said. "Al, take the orders if you would. We'll get a couple of buckets of soda. Okay? *Todos contentos y yo tambien*."

I have a little culinary rule, adopted after many years of traveling. The farther away you are from your dish's origins, the more likely it is to be sucky. Don't order a Philly Cheesesteak in Alaska. Don't order a Baked Alaska in Philly. Don't order a Western Omelette in Denver. Order a Denver Omelette. Don't order the Waldorf Salad in the Waldorf. Order the house salad, they invented it. And so on.

We all took somewhere between four and five minutes to get those sandwiches tucked away. Ain't much if you ain't Dutch, but this ain't bad either. Better than the Kaboose! "Onward," I commanded the driver.

"Okay, team," said the voice of the team captain. "We're going to work this off in the shootaround. And I don't want to hear any burping or farting now."

Bright lights, big city! The Paycock House of the University of Phillydelfidilly was right on one of those rivers in Philly, never could keep them straight. The wind from the river blew right through us and the gym was none too warm either, a real barn. But the ladies got warm during their shootaround. The Paycocks were at the other end, and they looked confident. That could work for us.

There was a commotion behind us and in trooped the Diametrics as promised, dragging their instruments, tying up their uniforms and wedging themselves into their corny hats. The cheer squad, five especially limber undergrads, three female and two male, ran down onto the court to cavort. There were Stan and Henry, the ringleaders. Henry had a young woman with him. She looked familiar somehow.

I walked over, and the band burst into a loud version of "Centerfield," I guess in honor of the coach. *Put me in coach, I'm ready to play. Ha, ha!* I quieted them with my hands.

"Don't I know you?" I said to the young woman.

"I'm Tanya," she said.

"Tanya the Goddess?" I said. Tanya had been the cheer captain of the 2012 Diametrics, an alluring figure to Monroe guys and gals alike. She had aged nicely.

She laughed and blushed. "Just a regular girl, sorry," she said. "I do miss the cheering, though. Congratulations, coach."

"Once a Diametric, always a Diametric," said Stan.

"Gay to woe, Henry," I said.

"I'm not gay," he said.

"No. I know," I said. "We have an epidemic of Wordback breaking out on the team. Backwards up the syllables to make new words. Way to go."

"Oh yeah, that corny shit they use on the Arkadelphia campus," he said.

"Is it any cornier than shizzle and finizzle?" I asked.

"I don't nizzle," he said. "I'll get yack to boo."

I laughed. "Do get mack to bee," I said.

"What's this about a new team song?" Stan said. " '1 Thing?' Do you know how hard that will be to do a horn arrangement for?"

“That’s what you do so well, maestro,” I said. “No more Raggedy Asses. We’re retiring that. I leave it to you.”

“Sheet it,” he said.

“We’ve got a game to win,” I said.

I was pretty confident we were going to surprise the preening Paycocks. The ladies had been sharp in practice and were full of sass and Philly cheesesteak.

“Put me in, coach,” Isabella said to me as I returned to the bench. “I’m ready to play.”

“We’ll see,” I said. “Gracie may need a rest, she’s been under the weather.”

Snap! Snap! Is the sound of our early going, crisp passes winding up in their intended targets. That and the squeaks of many sneaks, a sound I had grown to love. And the *blamming* of balls on the floor. Starbucks gets a threader and the big girl is laying it up to put us up. The next time they go down the corner I hold up two fingers. Sweet sees me and pulls up behind the line. 5-0. The Paycocks are rattled. DNA swipes and races down the court. 7-0. Next, Gracie scores from the top of the key and gets fouled. Timeout Paycocks. Isn’t there a Paycocks team at the University of Juneau too?

We’re just getting started. Vanessa C gets hot and I call plays for her. She outscores the Paycocks 8-6 over the next five minutes and our lead is 12. Sweet matches three Paycock buckets with two threes. I know how many fingers to hold up, I think.

The Diametrics are getting into it. They play “Momentum,” and “The Streets of Philadelphia.” The cheer squad does its “Hot Dog” sequence, which ends with the immortal phrase “Bite me!” Good choices! The half is winding down. We trade buckets with the Paycocks and at the end, Sweet bangs home a three at the buzzer. Unbelievably, we are up by 17 points.

“Okay,” I say in the visitors’ clubhouse to a happy and excited crowd, “let’s not get overconfident now. We still have

20 minutes to play. I'm going to start the Beeline and then bring you starters back later." The Beeline, the nonstarters, had been integral parts of the 2012 and 2015 squads.

"What's the good wordback," Al?" I say.

"Thuckfem," he says.

"Thuckfem it is." Except of course, it is us who are about to get thucked. The Beeline plays ragged, they haven't got the sharpness they should have, and the Paycocks are running over them. The opponents have the fire in their eye and when I pull the Beeline, our lead is down to six.

"Once more into the breach," I say to Sweet and Vanessa C as I put them back in.

"What that?" says Vanessa C.

"Poetry," explains Sweet.

The Paycocks kick it up a notch and despite Sweet and Vanessa C's snap passes they catch us up. Then they are up by two. Then they are up by four. Sweet gets knocked down and stripped of the ball. It is all slipping away. What can I do?

I get up and go over to the official. "Where's the call?" I ask. "Flagrant foul!"

The ref looks up to me. "You're crazy, coach," he says.

"You think I'm going to let my girls get knocked down because we're the visitors and the home team gets all the calls? NFW!" I say.

The ref looks at me. "Better go and sit down before you get a T, coach," he says. "Show me up and I'll throw you out of the game."

I turn and go back to the bench. I figure my side has seen me sticking up for them.

On the next possession, I can hear Sweet screaming at her teammates. It isn't it Wordback either. The Paycocks shoot and miss, there's a general rise for the rebound, and who comes down with it but Sweet, who at 5'6" is the smallest player on the court. She takes the ball all the way down the court and scores. And one! She pumps her fist.

Even with Sweet's heroics the Paycocks are game. As we go into the final minute it is tied. The Paycocks score. Sweet hustles back for a three. We're ahead with 30 seconds to go! The Paycocks play for the last bucket. Don't wait too long, ladies! Slowing down the tempo is rarely ever the right play. But, *oh no*! Their big girl is free in the paint. She gets the ball unopposed and rises for the jam. I close my eyes. I don't want to see this.

But wait! She's muffed the dunk, and the ball is coming back to the ground… the big girl gets the ball back and then Sweet steals it from her and dives to the ground with the ball under her. The buzzer goes off. Metrics by one!

"Seven to the Wreck!" I'm shouting. "Seven to the Wreck!" It's not a pretty win, but it's a win nevertheless.

The ladies have gathered in a crazycircle and are gyrating left and right as the rhythm of the world takes them. The Diametrics hustle onto the floor to play the Monroe Victory Song, something they haven't had much chance to do this year. The women stop twisting and put their hands on their hearts. Even I'm singing along to the ancient words.

"Onward, onward, old Monroe/ As we on to vict'ry go." Sweet song!

I look around for the media but there's no one there at all. No ESPN, no local news, no sports radio. We've been having too dismal a season to rate coverage. But I am happy anyway.

"The Metrics are back," I say to no one in particular.

As we were leaving the gym to get back on the bus for the ride back to New Netherlands, I had it underlined for me. It was only a fifty yard walk but that wasn't too short to show team pride.

"Sharpen up, Metrics!" came the voice of the team captain. "We're repping our college and our state here. What do we know?" Silence at this. "Hey Metrics, what do we know?"

"1 Thing?" said DVD.

"What do we know?" Sweet barked again.

"1 Thing!" This time everybody joined in.

The driver had come out after the game ended and started up the bus, so it was nice and warm in there against the winter night. I decided it was time to break some bad news to the team. Maybe I could make the pill go down easier.

"Okay, Metrics!" I said. "We won ugly, but we won. And we've won two in a row now." That matched the season high, actually. "So, good work. We're going on to Rochester to play the Shutters Sunday afternoon. Now, they've had a good season, and it's going to be on ESPN. The camera is going to be on the Shutters, not us"—I enjoyed the pun— "but let's turn that around. Let's get them interested in that 1 Thing we know that nobody else knows."

"What do we know?" said Starbucks, but someone slapped her arm.

"Here's the bad news, though," I said. "With budget cutbacks and all, they've cancelled our flight up there. We're going to have to take a bus."

"Not this stanky bus," Vanessa C said. "No way."

"No, I asked," I said. "A big cruiser, with movies and shows on demand. It's a long way to Rochester…"

"Where that?" said Starbucks. "Up in Canada?"

"Near Canada," I said. "But not Canada. New York state."

"We going to sleep in the bus?" came another voice.

"No," I said. "We got the Holiday Inn Supreme, right next to the Box." The Box was what they called Kodak's arena. "Al will handle the room list. Pair up or Al will do it for you. And we're leaving from the Zone at 3 PM sharp tomorrow. Don't be late."

Starbucks had another question. “Can we stop for another cheesesteak on the way back?”

It was dark when we got back to the Zone. A peaceful, cold, dark night. Absolutely no one living was in sight. The players ran for their cars, those who had them. Vanessa C threw down her bag in a fit.

“Damn boyfriend,” she said. “He better keep driving.”

The BF apparently hadn’t come to pick her up as arranged, or had been there but given up on us. Al Romero and I were walking up to this sorry scene.

“Al, we couldn’t even get mugged out here,” I said. “Vanessa C, hop in. Where to?”

“The Squat,” she said, naming the players’ living area and playhouse.

“Full service coach,” I said. “I’ll get you home.”

The Viet Cong have divided their forces. There is no way I can pirouette south the way I’d done once to elude them. There is only forward to go. When I look back I can’t see them in their black pyjamas, but I can see sunlight glinting from their mounted bayonets. It is rare they shoot me.

I come to a fork in the swampy trail, and I take it. I guess right turn, and soon I am huffing from climbing a steep hill. I hear the pinging of shots around me. Are the Cong worried I might get away? I push on even faster.

Damn! I come to the top of the hill and the end of the trail. I am on a bluff and there is a straight drop down of about 125 feet into the river.

I turn around. Now I can see the moving black spots, in two cohorts, coming up the hill for me. There is nowhere to go.

Bullets are best. They don’t like to waste them, so it is just sudden oblivion. The lukewarm slashes of the bayonets are the worst. When they drag me off for questioning, they don’t know I'll wake up before they get back to base, and I never tell them. But that has only happened once.

I look down at the river. Always did want to skydive once for the bucket list. This will be more like bungee jumping without a cord, but still. I draw myself up and lean forward.

Gravity takes over and I am falling, I can feel it in the pit of my stomach, falling without a parachute. But the river below is gone now and there is, what? Couldn't be, but it is. A basketball court, and I am falling on it from above. I have a basketball in my hands, and I am just about to make the first dunk of my life.

After I hit I tried to roll but got tangled up in something. What was it? Bed sheets! I was awake. Spotter was looking at me, her head tilted.

"Oh man!" I exhaled. "And one, Spotter! Flagrant foul!"

Spotter looked at me with puzzled eyes. My antic mood hadn't dispelled. "We'll talk more later," I said.

I'd gotten in after midnight. Dee was asleep. I'd turned the television on and conked. How I got to the bed I didn't know. I hoped my pregnant wife hadn't had to lug me.

"Dee!" I sang out. "I've got to pack. Back on the road already. This sucks! How do you put up with it?" But I got no reply. Dee had gone out.

I wrote her an incoherent note and then got ready for our trip to Rochester. I got to the Zone a couple of hours early, time to check the e-mails.

I was buoyed by the avalanche of congratulatory e-mails over our second straight win. Well, I would have, but there was only one. It was from the Scorpion.

"ESPN wants to interview u/ 1 of team before game," Scorpion said. "Nice win, btw!" Uh oh, would have to face the formidable Kara Lawson again. Well, I'll worry about that tomorrow, Scarlett.

Snow Angels

The bus was, as promised, a cruiser. We were all in on a cloudy day waiting to take off for Rochester. Weren't the days supposed to be getting longer now? I couldn't tell. The ladies were all zoned into their ear tabs or headsets, but Eddie, the driver, wasn't going.

"What's up, Eddie?" I asked.

"Coach, there's a foot in the door," he said.

So there was! Strange sight. Argyle sock too, looked like. Eddie opened the door again. The foot's owner promptly fell in a heap. I jumped up and went down the steps to him.

"Who are you?" I asked.

"M-M-Marvin," the young man answered. Looked like a student. Actually, looked like a band nerd, 2012 vintage before the Diametrics became cool. Ben Franklin glasses, shocky black hair.

"M-M-Marvin, what are you doing with your foot stuck in my bus?" I wanted to know, not unreasonably.

"I want to go with you to Rochester," he said.

"Why would you want to do that?" I said.

"I want to cover the team," he said. "For *The Rattler*."

Something didn't smell right about this. *The Rattler* was the daily student newspaper at Monroe/Sheridan City. If they wanted to go on the road with us, and nobody had wanted to in a while, they would have to get permission from the AD.

"What's the real story?" I asked. "I'm getting cold here."

"Okay, I'm not on the staff officially," he said. "But I want to be. You guys have won a couple straight and you're going to be on national TV tomorrow. I'm thinking there's a story there."

Many, many years ago I'd been a young reporter trying to hustle my way onto good stories. "Hop on," I said. "But don't make a fuss. Don't make me look bad. We're probably breaking all sorts of rules here."

Al Romero was giving the kid the beady eye when he got on. He pointed for him to sit across from Al in the second row. Then he stood up for his bus spiel.

"New Netherlands," he said, grandly. "When will we see again the great state of our birth, the first state to ratify the Constitution?"

"Shit gets old," the voice said, but Al didn't hear it.

"Uh coach?" said Marvin. "Could we swing by the Kaboose first? I haven't eaten all day."

"Marvin, maybe you will make a good reporter," I said. "Because you're a pain in the ass."

But the ladies had heard the exchange, and the chant came up: "Road food! Road food! Road food!"

"Let's go to Rochester," I told Eddie. "Via the Kaboose."

So I'm counting the cars on the New Jersey Turnpike again, as in the Paul Simon song, trying not to get hypnotized by the white stripes down the middle of the road. Al and Karla, sitting together, are dozing. Eddie, luckily, isn't dozing. The kid is wide awake.

"How old are you, Marvin?" I asked him. " 'Cause you look like you're sixteen."

"Eighteen, coach," he said. "I'm a freshman. Second term," he quickly added.

"Oh well, second term," I said, as if that gave him seniority. "You a fan of women's basketball?" I asked.

"Actually, I want to write about baseball," he said. "But I figure a game's a game. I know the rules, anyway."

"It helps to actually like the game you're covering," I said. "I covered baseball some. I covered both men's and women's basketball, and eventually I grew to like the women's game better than the men's."

"How come?" Marvin wanted to know. A good quality in a reporter, being curious.

"Well, you got no Shaqs, no Kobes," I said. "But you have much more of a sense of being on a team, of playing together. The men's game is too much jams and slams. Like baseball. You have homers, but you also have a game, and the one doesn't outshine the other. Can you imagine staying interested for 162 games if every one of them was a home run derby?"

"No," said Marvin. "But I could watch the first week the whole way through."

"I watch it once a year and it's great," I said. "But it's enough. So you don't have the exhibition game in the women's game. You have teamwork. But there's areas where the women are just as good as the men. In free throws, for instance, and in three pointers, and in sticky D. And if you believe Pip Pippen and the Big Girl, who are tearing it up in the WNBA, the women's game is just as good as the men's, or will be soon." Pip was the star of the Metrics' 2012 championship run, and the Big Girl was her nemesis from Constitution.

"Mind if I sit with you, coach?" Marvin asked. "You'll get a crick in your neck like this."

"Come on, then," I said.

Marvin carefully worked his way into the seat next to mine, negotiating the tremors of Eddie's driving. Eddie was like a reverse thoroughbred. He sped up when no one was in front of him. We were clocking about 80 now. But Rochester was a long way away.

"One of the things that made me want to do this is the fact that you were a reporter before you became a coach. Why the switch?"

I thought about it. "Change of life, really," I said. "When you're young you crave excitement and change. The game changes every time. You're in Cleveland. You're in Seattle. It's exciting the first few times around the circuit. And in baseball there's a rhythm. It's sweet, like the growing season. You start as winter is ending, and you end as autumn is knocking down the leaves. Baseball has life's rhythms. That's why people like it. And it's at its best in those hot, sweet days of high summer you never want to end."

"Very poetic," Marvin said. "I can see why they made you Poetry Coach."

"And basketball has rhythms, too. It starts after baseball, and stops just before opening day. So it's like the afterlife. Things die, and then they start to grow again. Who doesn't want to live again, Marvin? There's a real spiritual quality to basketball."

"A philosopher as well," Marvin said.

"Study Eduardo if you want to look at a real poetry coach," I said. "So I had all that. But then I started to want something different. A home life. A partner. A family. It hasn't been easy, but I'm working it through."

"But you're on the road right now," he said.

"Back home soon," I said.

"And if you're not coaching, your wife is," he said.

"We get to kiss between the raindrops," I said. "I'll always go back to her, back to Sheridan City."

"Is it true they have a Sheridan City in Jersey, too?" Marvin said. "I think I saw a sign for it back there."

"Well, maybe," I said. "There's a Las Vegas in New Mexico, too, but it isn't the bright lights-big city Vegas. Not that I'm ever going back to Vegas," I added.

"Never been to Rochester," Marvin said.

"Nothing wrong with Rochester," I said. "I used to see it when I was covering minor league baseball. Right on the lake, snows like a mother from the lake effect snow."

"I hear it's going to snow tomorrow," Marvin said.

"Well, we take the days as God gives them to us," I said. Crazy kid. Then I thought of something. "You got a place to stay in Rochester?" I said.

Marvin shook his head.

"You are a pain in the ass, Marvin," I said. "But I'm not going to let you sleep in the snow. You can bunk in with Al Romero. They have double beds."

"Thanks, coach," Marvin said. "One last question. What is this one thing you-all are supposed to know?"

"That would be telling, wouldn't it," I said.

We got in after midnight, and there were a bunch of grumpy athletes looking at me the next day when we got together in the lobby after breakfast.

"I like this change, ladies," I said. My players weren't wearing their usual loungewear, torn sweaters, stanky sneakers. They were glammed up nicely in couture clothing, suits, slacks, skirts. Not that I know fashion. But *haut couture* was a nice fit for *haut* tall women. They were breathtaking.

"How the heck--?" I was at a loss for words. "This must have cost a fortune."

"We want to represent on national television," Sweet said. "Didn't cost a thing. It was Sula's idea that we get loaner stuff for nothing. Cappie Pondexter is my hero, so I got in touch with her fashion company, Four Seasons Management. And here we are! Raggedy Asses no more."

"Smart," I marveled. "How did you make it work?"

"I prayed on it, coach," she said.

"But hey coach," Sula said. "If you get interviewed on ESPN, give them a shout out. Four Seasons Management."

"Great. Hope we can get the game in before the snow starts. Ladies, this is Marvin," I said. "He's with *The Rattler*. He came up here to cover the game."

"Better have something good to say if you write about us," Ursula said.

"What high school do you go to, Marvin?" came another wiseass voice. Carmen, maybe. It was the same voice each time, but it always seemed to come from different people.

"You want me to write something good about you, don't worry. My article will be good whichever way you play. But if you want it good the way you're talking, play sharp."

Good for you, Marvin, I thought. *Don't get too chummy with the team.*

"You're in for a treat, Reporter Boy," said Lara. "You picked the right bus to hitch a ride on."

That reminded me. I called Lara aside. From watching her in practice I thought she was ready to step up. She hadn't shown much earlier in the season, but it wasn't so long ago she was playing volleyball.

"Yeah coach," she said. She was tall and slender, both good for what I had in mind. Great for blocking volleyball shots, too.

"Great teams usually have a great sixth man," I said. "The job's open here. Beeline didn't show me much last game. Are you ready to step up? And can you play with Vanessa C?" I was remembering the bitch slapping between the two.

"I'm ready," Lara said. "Just one thing I can't figure, coach."

"What's that?" I wanted to know.

"Where's the net in this fricking game?"

"Right below the rim," I said. "That's where I want you to put it."

"Pretty small net," she faux-groused. A sense of humor! I liked that.

"Down here at noon," I said. "Our shootaround is at 1. Prime time is 2."

Damn! I was watching our shootaround at the Box, which was a short parking lot walk from the hotel. The ladies were in their white uniforms with royal blue striping, which they often wore on the road. Isabella could barely dribble with her good hand, but with her bad hand she was throwing fast, hard passes to her teammates. She bounced one off Ursula's shoulder and sent her staggering.

"Iz!" I called her in. When she trotted over, I said, "you ready to go?"

"I was born for this, coach," she said.

"I like what I see," I said. "I'm starting you. Don't hurt our players, though."

Getting close to game time. One of the ladies had brought speaker attachments to her MP3-er and was playing "1 Thing", the players bouncing up and down in three lines. They were loose and happy, and so was I. Diametrics in place? They'd rushed in late, but there they were.

Now I saw the ESPN producer waving at me briskly. We were definitely the second interview after the Shutters, who were ranked in the top 20 nationally. I waved to Sweet and we walked over to the producer, the cameraman, and the formidable Kara Lawson.

Only it wasn't Kara. But it was someone I knew. Venice Sanchez, a Tall Woman who had had one of the great WNBA careers after winning the 2001 NCAA title game with Notre Dame. She was also a sometime fan of the Metrics.

"We're on in 5,4,3," said the producer.

"I'm here with the new head coach for the Metrics, Nick Johnson," said Venice to the lens. "Not a great year so far for the Metrics," Venice said. "What's it going to take to beat the Shutters today?"

"Venice," I said, "if my players play the way they can, the final score may open a few eyes."

"Coach," she said, "your Metrics can be a surprising team over the years, winning in streaks and coming up with concepts like the poetry coach, the team theme song, some strange new lingo and the mission statement. Got a Monroe Doctrine this year?"

"Yes," I said. "It's simple. We're going to win every game the rest of the way out in the regular season."

"That's pretty ambitious, coach," she said.

"Two down, eight to go," I said.

"I see you've brought along the new team captain, Caroline Sweet. Sweet, I hear the team theme is Amerie's '1 Thing'. You were all dancing to it on the sidelines."

"That's right," Sweet said. "That's because there's one thing we know that nobody else knows."

"What's that one thing, Sweet?" Venice said. "From the cowboy movie?"

Sweet smiled, a crafty little smile for a woman of God. "Maybe I'll tell you sometime, Venice," she said.

"Tell me something in Wordback, Sweet. What's that all about?" said Venice.

"You switch around the syllables of phrases and make new words. Like I would say to you, have a date grey instead of have a great day.' "

Venice turned back to me. "Coach, I want to congratulate you on your basketball memoir that's just come out." She held the book up to the camera. "Really good book. I'm in it, too. It's called *The Very Best of Day and Night*. Pick it up. And good luck with the team, coach. When the Metrics get hot, they are the most exciting team in the conference."

"Thank you," I said. "It's a pleasure to talk to one of the all-time greats in women's basketball. Good luck with the broadcasting."

To my surprise, Venice gets a little misty. "I'll give it my best," she said.

Sometimes you're good, and sometimes you're lucky. I think I'm both that afternoon. The Shutters can't lay a hand on Isabella, and she zooms passes left and right, dribbles with either hand, and even slips through the paint to score a layup using the other hand if she can't find someone open. There seems to be an X drawn just under Sweet's ribcage that Iz finds again and again. She scores 14 points and has 14 assists, a team record for the season. Sweet scores 26. We are up by 12 at the half. The Diametrics are playing an original tune of Henry's on the court at halftime that I ask about later and find out it is called "*WTF*."

Basketball is a psychological challenge as well as a physical one, and I'm not going to make the same mistake I made against the Paycocks and be overconfident. The Shutters are a good team, a top 20 team, and they come out of the locker room with a hot foot. We are still playing well but our lead has dipped, first to 10, then to 8. Buzzer for the TV timeout.

"Lara!" I call. "You're going in for Gracie at forward." Gracie's energy is flagging and I am worried about her being sick.

Lara repays my confidence in her on the first play. I am about to call a play for her in Wordback but she beats me to it. She springs above everyone to wrestle down a rebound and then speeds up the court. The Shutters have gotten used to Isabella being the ballhandler and they blank out. Lara scores an easy layup. And on the next Shutter possession, she soars into the air to *smack!* The ball away from the net.

"See what a volleyball player can do, Al?" I asked.

"Fuckem," he agreed.

You ever see video where a guy leaps up, dunks, and shatters the backboard? I've never seen it done in the women's game but psychologically, Lara's three plays shatter the Shutters. She scores 10 more the rest of the way, blocks another two and when the buzzer goes off she is heading downcourt for another try, even though we are ahead by an unbelievable 20 points.

"Wicks to the Shreck!" I'm shouting. Hope I got that right.

This time, Venice interviews me first.

"You beat the Shutters convincingly tonight coach, with great games from Caroline Sweet, Isabella Matie and Lara Antipova, and you've won three straight. Are your Metrics back?"

"We'll take 'em one game at a time," I say. "But we'll be competitive in every game."

The Diametrics are pell-melling out onto the court in their inimitable fashion to play the Monroe victory song. Venice calls me back.

"Sign this for me, would you, Nick," she says, holding out the paperback of my book.

As the team showered and changed down the corridor, Al came in to my cubby in the visitors' area.

"I got good news and bad news," he said. "There's a shitload of snow coming down and even more to the east. The Thruway is closed. Eddie's dispatcher is telling him not to drive."

"How do we get home?" I asked.

"We don't tonight," he said. "The good news is, at halftime I called the hotel and booked us for another night just in case."

"Good man, Al," I said. "Dee isn't going to like this, but what can I do? You can bunk in with me," I said. "Eddie and Marvin can have the other coaches' room. Don't want him sleeping on the bus."

"Good thought," Al said.

"Now here's a little more bad news," I said to him. "I'm going to let *you* tell them we're not going home tonight."

The snow was coming down thickly as we walked out of the Box and into the emptied parking lot. The ladies were grousing.

"The Diametrics are on their way to the airport. They've got a flight. How come we got to stay another night and take the wiki bus back?"

"They're having a better year than we are," I said. "But we're turning that around now. Good work, ladies. Hey wait a minute. Stop. Listen to this."

We all stopped. It was the sound of silence we could hear, unless snow falling made some noise in some register we couldn't really hear.

"Is this a poetry moment?" Starbucks wanted to know. "Because it's pretty damn cold out here."

"It's February," I said. "Let's go with it." I reached down for some snow. It wasn't good packing snow. It was so cold the snow was dry like powder. I shoveled it at Starbucks.

Of course, I got it back in spades. And soon the team was happily pelting each other with the dry snow, chasing each other around the lot and shrieking. After a while I called the squad together.

"All right," I said. "Drop and give me snow angels!"

And the Metrics hit the deck and started waving their arms, making angels in the snow.

"Okay," I said, "snackaround is on me tonight."

That went over well. Snackaround was an important part of the daily life of the ladies. Perhaps even more than shootaround. They ate, usually together, a diet supervised by Karla, the trainer. So they ate really well. The trouble was, they got three meals a day and they needed four. So snackaround became a ritual, sometimes at the Kaboose, but usually at the team HQ, the Squat. And it involved the junkiest of comfort foods.

When we got back to the hotel it was bright and cheery. "Room service working?" I asked at the desk. "Hear there's 18 inches of snow coming."

"Piece of cake," the desk clerk said. "They may even not close the schools."

"Can I use your phone to call them?" I asked. Let's see. Pizza, definitely. Lots of pizza. Ribs, couple of racks. You do fried chicken up here in Lake Effect Land? Good. Two buckets. And sliders, we'll need a few plates of those. Mac and cheese? No? How about French fries then. Soda by the bucket. You have chocolate cake? We'll take the whole cake. Room charge, you bet.

There was a big table in the lounge where we spread out the snackaround when it came. There was a bright fire in the grate nearby and lo and behold, it was a real fire and not a fake one.

"Karla, you look the other way," I said to our trainer.

"Hell no," she said. "I'm looking at those ribs."

What we had left over wouldn't have made a midnight snack for two cockroaches. I felt real good feeding my snow angels, though I wondered if this would be considered reimbursable. Room service was outrageously overpriced. Still, any port in a storm.

There was a big window overlooking a deck. The lake was just beyond but we couldn't see it for the snow. It was still dropping straight down, very little wind. Eventually the sated team stood together, watching the snow outside through the window. Marvin and Eddie had vanished but the coaches were there.

"It's like Christmas Eve," said DVD.

"Do we get any presents?" asked Starbucks.

"Picture time!" said Vanessa C. Soon the ladies all had their phones out and were asking me to do a snaparound for them so they could upload them to their social media pages. You can see how happy a time that was from those pictures (the Internet is forever, right?). We were snowbound but warm and well fed, feeling the dizziness of a big win, being together with people we liked and respected. There was a word for it I couldn't put my finger on. Maybe it was the one thing.

Al Romero lugged his bag into my room and then excused himself. "You'll want to call home," he said. "I'll be downstairs." Al would be in the bar but I didn't begrudge him his tipple. Today was a day worth celebrating.

"I watched the game," Dee said when I got hold of her. "Nice move putting Lara in. The girl's starting to learn how to play basketball. I got so excited I thought the baby would drop right there."

"No babies can come unless I'm nearby," I said. "Which brings me to the bad news. We're snowed in. We won't be going home til tomorrow. Can you wait that long?"

"I'll have to be brave," she said. "Spotter will keep me company."

All of a sudden the exaltation of the win dropped away and I was sad. "I miss you already," I said. "I'm bunking with Al Romero and he hogs the covers."

"You leave Al alone," she said. "You bring it back to me."

Will do. I turned on the television and watched something without paying any attention. Then my phone rang. Dee calling me back. Great!

But it wasn't her. It was a voice I hadn't heard in a while, but was happy to hear.

"Nick, what you up to? You on ESPN, you knocking off a top 20 team, you talking about the one thing. You are sick, and I am glad."

"Julia!" I said. Lady Dagger. My best source on the Metrics when she played there in 2012 and 2013. Later my good friend.

"I thought it was March Madness when they named you coach, but you ripping it up," she said. "Proud of you, and tell the ladies the same. I give them some extreme poetry lessons every once in a while, you know. Proud alum."

"Will do," I said. "Where are you calling from?"

"Seattle," she said. "We're playing here tomorrow night." Dags played for San Antonio.

"It's snowing like hell here in Rochester," I said.

"We back on the road," she said.

"Only temporary for me," I said. "Just for a few games."

"How is Dee?" Julia asked. "When's the happy event?"

"Due date last week of February," I said. "She's doing fine. Baby's doing fine in the oven, far as the doctors can tell."

"Big doings," she said. "How you thinking about it, being a father?"

"Dags, since it's you I'll tell you. At first I was of two minds about it. But now I'm good with it. You know, you miss out on a lot when you're on the road all the time. I don't want to get cheated out of the big things in life."

"Soon as my career is over, me and Spo-kan Man are going to start making babies," she said. "He don't know it yet, but he'll be down with it. I'm not going to be on the road forever either."

"How long have you been in the league, Dags?" I asked.

"This is my fourth year," she said. "I figure maybe I'll play another five years, if I don't pop an ACL."

"And watch out for that meniscus," I said. I always liked the sound of that word.

"I'm not like Pip," Dags said. "She and the Big Girl, they're crusaders. Pip, she 90% basketball. I love basketball, but my percentage is a lot lower."

"Great to hear from you, Dags," I said. "I think it's a boy. But if the baby is a girl I'll name her after you."

"Miss Dee might have something to say about that," Julia said. "But I'm making a note of that due date."

Rochester was teeming with snow the next morning, but it had stopped falling.

"When's the next storm?" I asked the front desk clerk.

"They're saying tomorrow," she said.

"Eddie, you have to get us home between the snowflakes," I said to our driver.

"When do you want to go?" he said. Good man!

"Wake Marvin up," I said. "I don't want to leave his skinny ass behind."

Once we were back on the bus I called Dee. "Coming home today," I said. "But I don't think I'll be home for dinner."

"I'm going to hold you to it for tomorrow," she said.

"Write me in," I said.

Upstate New York looked great encased in snow. The farther south we got, the less snow there was. By the time we got to the New Jersey Turnpike, the ground was clear.

I looked behind me. Most of my rim warriors were sleeping peacefully. Marvin was banging out his story on a laptop with a little laser light attachment so he could see. Hope he didn't get seasick easily! I debated counting the cars again but then I must have fallen asleep because it was dark and cold from the open door and we were in the parking lot at the Zone. I was back home and I was ready to go back home.

This time, we had a small crowd waiting for us. BFs and GFs of the team, and some for the Diametrics, whose plane had been cancelled and were coming back by a hastily chartered bus. There was a smattering of applause for us as we got off the bus.

“Hold on to your wallet, coach,” said Al Romero. “Looks like you could get mugged tonight.”

Dark As a Black Steer's Tookus

The next day at work my computer was flush with congratulatory messages. And why not? We'd beaten a top-20 team by 20 points on their own court. We'd been on ESPN and interviewed by the great Venice Sanchez. But those weren't the only reasons.

E-mails titled "Great Win!" were alternating with "Great Story!" What great story? I opened a couple. They were raving about Marvin's story in *The Rattler*!

How in the heck did he ever make the deadline for today's paper? Then I remembered: this year *The Rattler* was totally online. No more killing trees. Only pixels would have to be consumed.

Naturally, first I read every congratulatory e-mail. Some of them were heartwarming, especially alums. The great Pip Pippen wrote me one. So did Penthouse, whom I'd helped make a key pronouncement on ESPN back in 2015. OMG. Here was one from Geno Auriemma!

"Glad we don't have to play you in the regular season," Geno wrote. "LOL! See you in the Beast." Well, I appreciated even jokes from the great Geno. I was trying to win ten in a row. He'd won 90 in a row with UConn.

Okay, let's go online and see what the heck the kid wrote. Rattler.com, it's coming up. (By the way, the name of the paper has nothing to do with snakes, though they do call their clubhouse The Snakepit. Apparently the paper used in the first editions more than a century ago was so crisp it kind of rattled when the pages opened. Oh, the vanishing elegance of print!)

Spawts, as the clever lads and gals there titled the section. There it was. "On the Bus with the Metrics," was the hed, next to a photo of the SceniCruiser he'd taken with his telephone. "I knew it was going to be a long, strange trip when the door of the SceniCuiser closed on my foot," it started. We didn't lead sports stories like that back in the day! But it was a different day.

It was a lot longer story than I used to write, too, when I was covering the Metrics. I scrolled down and saw there were four pages to it. Why, it must be 3,000 words! More like a short story than a newspaper article (or content, as it's now known).

But was I surprised! The story was sweet, wise, smooth as silk. I didn't as much as breathe while I read it. Marvin was a quick study. Everything was in there. Gassing with the players on the bus, gassing with me (he even mentioned my book), the Diametrics, Venice Sanchez, the wordback, the 1 Thing, the big win, the snow angels (he must have been watching from the hotel lobby), the snackaround, he got everything in. With pictures and video! There was even a link to Amerie's video. A handsome woman, Amerie.

Here's how Marvin's story ended. "When we get back, it is, as in the Coen Brothers' movie, dark as a black steer's *tookus* on a moonless prairie night. We're not on the prairies, but with the wind and cold it feels like it. More like the steppes. And there's no way to tell what the end of the story will be. But for now, we have eluded the partisans, and are making our way home through the dark and the snow."

I looked up, and there was Al, holding what I could see was a printout of the article.

"Did you see this?" he asked. "Kid can write."

"Yeah," I said. "I think we found our poet for the team, Al. And with Lara as sixth man, everything is falling into place. We could actually do this."

"This isn't poetry," Al said. "It's sports."

"But he gets it somehow. What Pip once said about me, tapping the Stephen King movie. He has the shining. He can see us. This thing of ours. How he gets it, I don't know. Maybe he's a genius or something. It's poetry."

"Well, you were the poetry coach last time so you should know. Let's get him back for our next game," Al said.

"Wait a sec, wait a second," I said, looking at my computer screen. "I've just gotten an e-mail from the provost!"

"Enjoyed the content on the team in *The Rattler*," it said. "Who is Marvin Holsapple? Good the Metrics are shaking it up again. My best to Dee. Don O'Malley."

"Provost Don," Al said, admiringly. "Maybe we'll get hired back for next year."

"Not me," I said. "I'm just keeping the seat warm for Dee. She'll be coaching next year."

"Somebody will be here," Al said. "Or in the new Wreck I mean. Meanwhile what play you want me to drill the ladies on?"

"The rick and pole," I said.

"Rick and pole. Gotcha," Al said.

Time to get serious about our next game. Get video on them, study their offense, their defense. On the other hand I hadn't looked at any film yet. Maybe it would be bad luck!

What could I do to beat St. John's tomorrow night? Well, one thing was playing the hot hand. I didn't care if it was the water boy (of course we didn't have a water boy). And then the reverse. How many times did a player score 18 in the first ten minutes and then one the rest of the way? I'd milk the player for her 18 and then sit her down.

I became aware there was a Tall Woman in my small room. I looked up. It was Ursula, and she had something in her hand.

"Sit down, Ursula," I said. "You played some good minutes against the Shutters." Ursula was just the kind of player to put in when your big scorer went cold, scrapped for every ball. She smiled at the praise.

"Marvin said I played like I wasn't afraid for my life," she said. "It's in *The Rattler*. Pretty good."

Marvin. I was getting a little jealous of Marvin. Maybe I should just let Marvin coach, I thought. Doogie Howser, Division I Coach.

"Got some bad news, coach," she said. She held out something she had in her hand. A letter.

I knew what it was, though I'd never seen one before. It was a Wells letter, a notice of academic insufficiency. Put you on notice you were ineligible to play unless you cleared the deficiency within a week.

"What's it for, Sula?" I asked.

"Philosophy," she said. "Don't know why I have to take it. I'm a business major."

I started to launch into an explanation of the rationale behind a humanities education but then decided against it.

"Can you get a tutor?" I asked.

"Nuh," she said, shaking her head. "None available now, they told me."

"Well, I can scout around," I said.

"Please coach," she said. "I don't want to lose my scholarship."

"Okay," I said. "Maybe I could help. I took philosophy in school. Maybe there's something still back there in my head about it."

"Okay," Sula said. "Can you come over to the Squat tonight? Cause I got an exercise due Thursday."

"My wife will kill me if I'm not home for dinner tonight," I said. "But maybe I could come over about nine."

Dee gave me an A for effort for being home as promised. But she wasn't thrilled about my visit to the Squat.

"How's your arm?" she asked. The bandage was coming off tomorrow. "Let's see. You already took a bullet for the team. I grant you, tutoring Kant is a lot less dangerous. But let me suggest something. I know you love the ladies. It's an endearing thing you have. But don't get too close to them. You're their coach, not their big brother. Don't let the lines get too blurry. It won't be any good."

My wife is awfully smart. A lot smarter than I am. "You're right," I said. "Let me go this time, because I promised. But this will end my academic career."

I'd never been to the Squat before, even though it was only half a mile or so from the Wreck. It wasn't what I expected. From the name I thought it would be a dank place with jock boxes (pizza) all around and the smell of old beer. But it was scrupulously neat (there was a system in place, and fines for noncompliance) and kind of comfortable. There was a big common room that had a study area with a couple of PCs, some foamy old chairs in front of a wide screen TV, and even an exercise corner with three or four torture machines. There were Metrics basketball photos framed on the wall. Dags, Pip. Horse and House. Nice. In the center was a big table that could seat eight. The remains of the snackaround were there, along with some stained Kaboose bags. Doors at regular intervals led to the four bedrooms. If any of the players went into the bedrooms with a guy or even another gal and turned the music up, I'm not going to say.

"Help yourself, coach," said Carmen, who'd hopped off a machine to let me in and then hopped back on, virtuous sweat on her face. "We're all stuffed."

It's true the ladies were prodigious eaters, but there wasn't a fat molecule between them. Between the stressful hustle of college life and the arduous regimens of basketball, they were bottomless pits for both healthy and junk food. Plus, they were young.

"No thanks," I said. "Just ate."

Vanessa C. and DVD were watching reality TV. Sula was over at one of the PCs. She had a worried look. "Here's my exercise," she said. "Compare and contrast the ideas of Hegel and Kant. See how they are congruent and incongruent. I looked up congruent. It means, like the same as."

"Okay," I said. "Let's go to the Internet. Nothing on the Internet is ever wrong. Maybe we'll get lucky." I typed the exercise into a Google query and boom, there was a guy talking about this very topic.

"Write this down," I said. "Guy says it's a trick question. It doesn't make any logical sense."

"Alright," Sula said, "but none of it makes sense. I don't see why I have to do this philosophy stuff. I'm never going to use it in real life."

"What do you want to do in real life, Sula?" I asked.

"Finance," she said. "I'll never make the WNBA so I need the degree. Look here." She whipped through a few keystrokes and there was a balance sheet for the Squat. The numbers looked impressive.

"I did an analysis and I was able to save enough from the budget to get a cleaning lady in here every day," she said. *That's* why it was so clean!

"Looks good," I said. "Okay! Let's get you a degree. Let's look into the problem a little more in case Philosophy Geek is wrong."

I applied myself to the PC. But soon I was all in a tangle. I had to look up some big words and then when I did I couldn't get back to my original pages. Where was the back button on this *ficacta* machine? Oh boy. I was thinking the only Nietzsche I knew anything about was the old Green Bay football player.

"Getting there, getting there," I said to Sula after about fifteen minutes. I got no response. When I looked up I saw she was peacefully dozing with her head on her arms.

I need help here, I thought to myself. Sweet and Izzy came in in sweats and I waved to them and they waved back. They headed for the machines.

How did Littlejohn do it? I asked myself. Bet he saw a ton of Wells letters in his day. But about 90% of his women graduated. What was his formula?

The light bulb went on. I pulled out my cell and dialed a number I'd called a million times when I was writing a book on him.

"Coach," I said. "Not too late to call? I've got a problem."

"That Nick?" he said. "Congratulations. Meant to call but I've been away for a week. Playing golf where it's warm. I'm way too busy in retirement."

"I need a favor," I said.

"Forget it," said Littlejohn. "I'm not coming back."

"That's not it," I said. "I've got a Wells letter for one of the women. How did you handle it?"

"Well, I coached forty years. I know a million people."

Sure, I thought. The point?

"What subject?" he asked me.

"Philosophy," I said.

"Just a minute," he said. "Searching, searching…" I didn't have a clue where this conversation was going.

"Got it," said Littlejohn. "Here's a name and number. Dr. Armand Frankfurter. Doctor of Philosophy here at Monroe. Owes me a couple of favors." He paused a moment, still reading, apparently. "Look here. Pulitzer Prize for his latest book. I should think he'll do?"

"Boy howdy," I said. I paused. "Coach, how did you ever do it for so long? It's like there's a crisis every day."

"I loved it," he said. "You just take it as it comes. You gotta love it or you stop coming in to work. I've seen you at work, son, writing and being a coach. You love it. Dee loves it."

"Not all of it," I said. "Thirty-nine years. Any regrets?"

I heard Littlejohn's breath come out. "I regret you got hurt," he said. "I regret Daria got hurt."

Damn! Didn't need to think about that again. "Not your fault, Coach. I'm younger than you, faster. I was the logical one to go in after her."

"Yeah," he said, unconvinced. "You call Dr. Armand. He'll bring your girl up to snuff. I've got a lot more good names if you have this problem again. It's important. Make sure they stay in school after March Madness, take their finals. There's a bright line in the workforce, and it's that college degree. Above, good. Below, bad. I always loved it that I trained ballplayers who became doctors, nurses, accountants."

"I'm with you," I said.

"Wait a second," Littlejohn said. "I see it here. Dr. Armand. He won the Nobel Prize too."

"That'll do," I said.

"You want to play golf, you give me a ring," he said.

I got off the phone. DVD looked up from the TV as I was writing down the name and number for Sula. "She always studying," DVD said, nodding at Sula. "I don't know why she doesn't get straight 4.0s."

"It's like basketball," I said. "Some people are born athletes. Some people are born scholars. Other people have to hustle after it. Sula, she's got the drive both ways. And let me tell you something, D, and pass this along to the other ladies: it doesn't matter if you get all Cs. No one will ever ask you what your GPA was. They'll ask if you have a degree or not."

"Phys ed, that's me," DVD said. "Not so hard for me."

“What are you going to do if you don’t make the WNBA?” I asked.

DVD shrugged her shoulders. “Teach?”

“Good answer,” I said.

The Ice Cream Strategy

The wolves are close. There is snow and bitter wind. Famine in the woods, and the wolves are starving. No mercy will be shown. What's the point of running? Maybe I can get to the house I'd seen last time. I struggle on, a flimsy rag in front of my face, like Zhivago coming home in the deep freeze.

There it is! The house. I can tell, though, from the sound of the barking behind me, I'll never get there. Just like last time.

Then the door to the house bursts open and something springs out and starts sprinting for me. Another wolf! No, no, it's Spotter!

Go back, girl, I think. *No sense in both of us dying*. But Spotter keeps on coming and dashes past me, giving me a sidelong look that says, *get into the house. No sense both of us dying.*

I turn and watch her hurl herself at the alpha male. Horrible snarling ensues. I hesitate a moment but the other wolves are splitting into threes, one to help the alpha male and one to hunt me down. I turn and flee into the house, locking the door and looking horrified out the window as three large *thumps* make the door shudder.

The wolves try again, ramming the door with all their might. Then they sniff around the bottom of the door and lope off again. The sounds of fighting cease.

After a bit a lone form comes walking toward the house. It is a red wolf, something I've never seen before. Then

I realize to my horror it is Spotter, covered in blood. How has she stood off six wolves? But she has.

I open the door and she labors in, collapsing. I pick her up in my arms and turn around. I am center court at the Wreck, the new one. The house is full of silent fans watching us. I look around, and the ref comes out to take Spotter out of my hands.

"Great effort, coach," the ref says. And I see the ref is Dee.

I sat straight up in bed. How did my bed get into the Wreck? How did the Wreck get into my house?

Things sorted themselves out. I was weeping, quietly so as not to wake Dee. Then something occurred to me. Spotter wasn't dead, at least not in this dream world I'd woken up into. The tears dried and I got out of bed.

"Nick?" said Dee. "You okay?"

"I'm alright," I said.

"Where in the world are you going?" she asked.

"I'm going to check on Spotter, she if she's okay," I said.

"What?" she said. "Of course she's okay. Come back to bed. The strange things you get into your head sometimes."

I got back into bed. *Note to self*, I thought. *Stop in convenience store for doggy treats.*

The next day I had another 50 congratulatory texts or e-mails. And this time, they were all about Marvin's article. We'd gone viral in a moderate way, it seemed. One of the e-mails was from Kuala Lumpur (not quite sure where that is). Some story about a will, and money to be retrieved from an account in the US. Sounded like easy money! Aggregator sites had linked to the article. My phone lines (I had all of two) were flashing nonstop. Not that I'd picked the phone up once. I was trying to figure out St. John's in time for tonight's game in the Zone. The Red Storm had a proud tradition and a fine record this year. They would not be pushovers.

I decided to go home for lunch. I was a little spooked.

"Dee, it's getting weird," I said to my very pregnant wife. "We go from ignored to being a big thing on campus."

"Don't worry," she said over our tuna salad. "Enjoy it. Basketball is manic, you know that. You have to be nerveless. If you tense up, if you get the yips, the whole bubble will pop."

"What are the yips?" I asked. I knew what they were but Dee was in a talkative mood. She'd spent a lot of her pregnancy looking inward. I liked to draw her out.

"Big game nerves. Lid on the bucket. What drops at the shootaround clanks out in the game."

"Let's get out the board," I said. I'd grown to love to play checkers with Dee even though she beat me all the time.

"Spotter!" I said as the dog came into the room. She trotted over to me to be petted. "Don't mess the board," I warned the dog.

"What were you on about Spotter last night?" Dee said. "Sleepwalking?"

"No," I said. "Wolf dream. This time Spotter defended me and saved my life, but she was covered in blood."

"Horrible," she said. "Want a valium?"

"Not taking anything," I said. "Going with what God gives me."

"The team will be good for you," Dee said, making the last move. "Throw yourself into it and you won't have time to be thinking about other things. And they'll shrink and go away."

"Hope so," I said, settling into my easy chair after losing. "Sleeping has been hard for me."

Famous last words! I woke up next when Dee shook me and said I shouldn't miss the game, a real coach no-no. I'd been asleep for two hours. But I hadn't dreamed. I felt safe and warm where I was, with Dee. But I also felt the draw of the team, the game, the hoopla.

"I'll be back as soon as I ever can," I said to Dee as I left.

I had an hour or so before the game so I put through a call to the rehab. When I explained who I was they said I could have five minutes with Earlene.

"Coach," she acknowledged me.

"How are you, Goat?" I asked.

"They're giving me a cane," she said. "I might be able to walk tomorrow."

"What about the rest?"

"I feel terrible, coach," she said. "There's no end to feeling bad here. But I want to thank you. You really pulled me out of the firing line. You took a GSW too? My bad. I feel that's on me."

"Don't you worry about that," I said. "Look, I've been through the same thing you're going through. Actually I was at the same rehab you are. They still got those curlicue flower paintings on the wall? We used to cut out paper flowers and tape them to the paintings to see if anyone would notice. Different addictions, but you know they are all the same thing in the end. You believe you can't live your life the way God made you. You think you need help, you need excitement, you need to ease your pain."

"We go over this, every freaking day, three times a day," she said.

"You got to learn your lesson," I said. "Can't do that at a spa and resort. Will it get better right away? Probably not. But it will get different. And then it's up to you to choose what to do."

"Can I play basketball?" she wanted to know.

"I hope so," I said. "You're right up there with the best. You have to be clean and sober. You won't get a third chance either. And listen, Goat, I want to shake you. You're on a team. You're surrounded by people who care for you and want to help you. What the fuck are you doing sinking back into your shell, taking performance-destroying drugs? You were disrespecting the team."

"I been asking that myself," she said.

"Keep asking," I said.

"You won a couple," she said.

"Yeah," I said. "And tonight we're going to play for you, Goat. Tonight we're going to win for you."

The ladies were up for it when they crowded into my little cubby ten minutes later. Some of them just couldn't fit in, so they stayed out in the hall.

"Never going to believe this, coach…" said Starbucks, but I put up my hand.

"I just talked to Earlene, and I told her we were going to win tonight for her. So here's what I want you to do, to keep the Goat in your minds. Every time we score, I want the bench to say "Earlene," I said. "And I want to hear it a lot."

The ladies all put their hands together. I put my hand on somebody's back, to get into the energy.

"Earlene!" they said, and broke.

As I followed the team out towards the tunnel to the arena floor, I heard a noise coming from the coaches' bathroom. Shouldn't be anyone in there unless it was one of us.

The sound of retching assaulted my ears. It wasn't one of the coaches. A basketball-shorts-wearing rear end was backed out of the stall. I thought I recognized who was making the noises.

"Gracie, that you?"

"I'll be aight, coach," she said. "Give me a few minutes and I'll be right out."

Holy cow! Our gym was filled with people making noise. And there were the Diametrics, on time and the best noisemakers in the basketball universe. And there were the bright lights that banished depression. And there was half my life. And I started to smile, and kept on smiling when Brad cued up "1 Thing" in the booth so everybody in the hall could jump up and down in place. And we had press- there was Marvin in his Union-side Civil War cap and the beat reporter for the local news website, who hadn't been to the last 14 Metrics games.

I'm smiling all the way through our fourth consecutive victory. The Reds are a good team but they came here on the wrong night. The ladies start chanting "Ear-lene!" on every goal they make in the shootaround, the "ear" part when they shoot, the "-lene" part when it drops.

Our center, Starbucks, opens hot. She's got 12 points in the first five minutes. Six "Earlenes!" from the bench. She looks like a combo of House, the Big Girl, and Jayne Appel. Add in a little Toni Braxton. But when the shots start bouncing out, I sit her down and send Lara in.

"You'll hot up again," I tell her when, miffed, she comes in and sits down. "Earlene! And you'll go back in."

Lara is more naturally a forward than a center, so her game is to start a triumvirate of three forwards—herself, Vanessa C, and DVD, and do a Big Girl Push. They crash every board, camp out in the paint just shy of getting called, even let loose a bunch of threes. And they get fouled about four times each.

We're up by 14 with two minutes to go in the half. The ladies slow it down to chew up the clock, and I'm up from the bench shouting at them to speed it up. Nothing worse than for a team to lose a successful rhythm by stalling. So they do, and score two buckets while the Reds' two shots clank out. We're up by 18 in a delirious Zone.

"Lara, beautifully done," I tell the team in the clubhouse for the half. "Earlene! Now I'm sure Starbucks has waited out her cold streak, so she's going back in. Don't let up, keep them guessing, tonight is our night!"

The Reds don't know what hit them when our natural stars, Sweet and Izzy, finally get hot. Starbucks is a rebounding machine shoveling out lead passes to our guards, and they're galloping down the floor and zapping each other with miracle passes time after time. When the Reds call time out with five minutes to go, we are up by 30 points. I can't believe it. We've blown them out of the barn. I have to hide my head in a towel. Earlene! This one is for you.

Why an unranked team has to show props to a top-20 team by not showing them up is a mystery to me, but it's a tradition and I'm all over traditions. In goes the Beeline, Lara and Ursula and Carmen, Roshonti and a semi-recovered Graciela, to knock the rust off. We win by 20 and it's like a tickertape parade in the Zone. We've knocked off two top 20 teams in just a couple of days by 20 points each. Suddenly Geno doesn't seem so out of reach anymore.

There's Marvin, with his tape recorder, darting around the pack of Tall Women looking like the runt cub trying to get in to the tit. "Marvin!" I call out. "You got All Access, all the time. You need a quote? I'm a Quote Machine today. Did we give you any poetry tonight?"

"I think I can get something out of this, coach," he says.

Well, at least the uncertainty factor is gone. When I get to the fork in the swamp, I go to the left. The right leads to certain death over the cliff. I hear a stutter of automatic rifles and the leaves are being clipped off the trees and swampstuff above, but not missing me by much. I run faster.

Running downhill! Excellent. That should get me to the river. Give it a try, why not? More *brap-brap-brap*, one of the bullets singes me on the arm just above my horse tattoo. There isn't any more time.

The river bank! I leap into the water and start swimming upstream, to throw them off. I've just paddled around a muddy bend when I hear the Viet Cong reach the river bank and start to argue. One of them looses a prophylactic burst of gunfire into the water downstream, but I'm not there. I'm treading water and trying not to be washed downstream and into their view by the current.

Wait! Something is floating down the river towards me. It's a big log, looks as if it came off a ship or something. When it reaches me, I grab on and use it to shield myself from the bank. Just as I roll into their sight the VC start trotting off downstream, firing into the river at intervals in case I might be under water.

Damn. I'm floating at about the same pace as they are walking. I hear their voices, arguing. The water is too deep for me to stand up, I have to sail with the current.

This goes on for a very nerve-wracking mile or so. Finally, the VC seem to give up, but they don't move off. They are squatting by the river's edge, looking downstream. I'm clinging to the log but drifting into their view.

The water starts churning all around me. I lift my body up along the log to avoid water strafing. They are using the enormous log as target practice. But it is an easy target, and after a little while they stop. And after another little while, they get up and vanish back into the jungle.

I float farther down the river. It is so quiet and peaceful. And warm. I notice something strange. The log I'm clinging to is warm. *Very warm.*

One eye opens. I have both my hands on the warm body of my wife sleeping next to me. I close the eye again, but I don't let go. I sleep again. The only thing I dream of now is of my wife's body that I cling to in the muddy river, holding me safe from all harm in the bobbing waters.

One hundred fifty congratulatory e-mails the next morning at work. Of course the biggest impression I got was that it was Marvin who was responsible for the win with his content "At Home with the Metrics." But he wrote it beautifully. He even got the *"Earlene!s"* in the right places. I couldn't be jealous. I had to savor every word.

At practice I was feeling something was off. We actually had people in the stands at the practice, and that wasn't usual. It was throwing the ladies off. Passes were going out of bounds. Threes were hitting nothing but nothing. The rim had a covering made of steel.

I had a thought. I scooted back to Al Romero's cubby, where he kept his golf bag in order to minimize time between the end of practice and the first tee. He even played in the winter, using a golf cart with a bun warmer. I took out the putter.

Back in the arena I walked onto the court and called a halt to the practice. The ladies looked at me funny. I'd never walked out to them with a golf club before.

"Don't beat us, coach," said a voice. "We'll get better!"

"Important demonstration for you," I said to them. "Watch me closely." And I mimed lining up a putt and hitting it.

"Did I make the putt or did I miss it?" I asked them. The team looked at me blankly. "It was a three footer, an easy putt. Anybody? No? Well, I'll tell you. I missed this easy putt. And why?"

"They moved the imaginary hole?" said the smartass voice.

"Nothing to do with the hole," I said. "I've got a case of the yips. The yips is what makes you miss an easy putt. You get nervous. Your muscles clench. You get an adrenalin spike. And the swing you programmed into your head is not the one you actually swing. Here's the point. I'm watching you. There's people all around. The media is calling you and texting you. You're reading your names on the websites. This thing of ours used to be just us. But now we're hot. And you're rattled, pardon the pun. You've got the basketball yips."

"How do you fix the yips?" came the voice, not smartass this time but on the level.

"Bad news is there's nothing you can do physically," I said. "It's an emotional thing. You have to relax. You have to go back to the way you were before. If you have a reset button, ladies, I suggest you press it now. If not, I have another strategy."

"What that?" said a voice.

"When Venice Sanchez was interviewing me and Sweet I was thinking back to the first time I met her. She gave us some advice and somebody asked her, well, what if that doesn't work. And she said, 'well, you can always get some ice cream.' "

Silence. The voice said "Mr. Dee got the mental yips today."

"Here's what it is," I said. "We're done for the day. Hit the showers. And then, who am I to be smarter than the great Venice Sanchez, I'm taking the whole team out for ice cream."

"That might do it!" said the voice. "Cream Concoctions!"

While I waited in my office for the ladies (Al had gotten his putter back, plus an early start for golf and the 19th Hole bar), I had an unexpected visitor. The Scorpion.

"Just wanted to say good job," Scorpion said, holding out his hand, which was big for him because he was phobic about germs. "I think you may be getting the team ready for the Wreck faster than I'm getting the Wreck ready for the team."

"Still got a few games to play first," I said. "You still got time."

"You got the number for AAA?" the Scorpion said. "My clunker of a car has conked out again." Just then the AD's phone rang. He took the call and listened for a minute, then passed the phone over to me and said "Emory."

Emory? Weren't they Division III? We had to get an exception even to play a Div II team like Kill van Kull. Forget Div III.

"Yello," I said. I listened for a few moments and then I said, "Wow, great to hear from you. I'd love it. You had it right the first time. The AD would set this up with you. Let me pass you back to him." Scorpion took his phone back and wandered down the hall, looking for better reception.

"Okay, coach, see you," said Karla, coming by.

"Want to come for ice cream, Karla?" I said. It bothered me that I didn't like to talk to Karla. It was no fault of her own.

"Diet, sorry," she said. "I'll see you tomorrow for gameday, coach."

"Karla," I said. "You're doing a fine job. Anything you need, equipment, supplies, you come to me for it."

"Fax me over a Mocha Hoka," she said, smiling. "No reason I can't look at it."

Sheridan City boasted one of the best independent ice cream parlors in the country. Cream Concoctions on Acquakanonk Ave. had lines snaking out of it even during the rain, sometimes even in winter. Luckily we didn't have to wait that February day, though the place was nearly filled. Ice Cream Fountain Mountains washed down with diet sodas were the order of the day (no contradiction, by the way).

"You girls are awful tall," said the counter man. "Are you the Monroe Metrics?"

"You got it," I said.

The counter man raised his voice. “Hey everybody,” he said. “We got the Monroe Metrics women’s basketball team in the house that’s been tearing up the league.”

Cheers and clapping for the Monroe Metrics, us! From every one in the store. I even got a little emotional. A little girl came up shyly with something to sign and every one of the Metrics signed it while we waited for our orders.

“This is who we play for, ladies,” I said. “Not ESPN, not the sports websites. This feels good.”

“Ram date,” said Sweet.

The little girl came up to me. “Will you sign this, coach?”

“I’d be glad to,” I said.

“Yank thew,” she said.

Who isn’t happy eating ice cream? Silly season didn’t start until the Fountain Mountains crumbled to the sea. Then the gals with straws started zinging each other with spitballs. I might have even felt one my way. Then they started snapping each other’s photos with their cell phones. When Sweet got jostled and fell to the floor, three of the women dived for her cell. Then ALL the rest of them piled on, laughing like Monty Python Vikings eating Spam.

I had to take a photo of this Metrics pileup with my own cell phone. Then I made an announcement.

“Ladies, I think the yips are officially banished.”

The Stony Brook team is called the Sea Wolves. I don’t remember an animal called a sea wolf, but with my recent dreams I don’t like to be reminded. I want to send the pack of them back to Long Island ASAP. I’m looking at the Beeline just before the game. Who’s going to step up this night if the yips return for the starters? Carmen? Roshanti? Amazing Graciela is standing against the lights so there’s a glow around her. Must be a sign, right? I’m going with it.

"Gracie!" I say. "You feeling okay? Stay warm. You're starting the second half."

"Thanks coach," she says. "You won't be sorry."

"What's the good word, Al?" I say to my coach, though I already know what it will be.

"Fuckem!" he says. But then he surprises me, with a second word.

"1 Things!" he says. And then, unprecedented, a third.

"Monroe Metrics, from the great state of New Netherlands!"

The gym is full of people and energy. The Diametrics are playing "Sweet Caroline" in honor of Caroline Sweet, who actually doesn't like that song much but is too polite to say so to Stan and Henry. Besides, some other sports team uses it.

I look up to Brad in the AV room and give him the high sign. "1 Thing" starts cranking, and this time the folks in the stands seem to be familiar with it, juking to the ancient and honorable beat of the go go.

Starbucks wins the tip and taps it to Vanessa C, who takes it down the court and lays it up. But that 2-0 is going to be our only lead of the half. The Sea Wolves break big and soon have us down by 2, 4, 6. Looks like the yips to me. Time out, me. I'm going to mix it up.

"Roshanti!" I say. "Go in for Starbucks. And Carmen, go in for Sweet."

I don't think we ever played or even practiced with this lineup before, and my hunch here is a bettor's hunch, one that seems sound at the time but is disastrous in hindsight. Roshonti is the tallest girl on my team, and big around too, but she's a freshman and unused to the sharp elbows and hip shoves she's getting. Twice she spills to the floor. We are down by 8, 10, 12.

"Caro and Star, back in," I say. But their time on the bench hasn't banished the yips. We are down by 14, 16, 19 (a three). Time out, me. I don't know what to do. I decide to phone a friend. We aren't on national TV but we are streaming live over the Internet, so Dee is watching.

"You must be tripping because you never called me for advice before," she says. "I was starting to think I must be a sucko coach or something."

"The team's got the yips like you said," I say. "We should be beating these Sea Wolves but we're way too anxious. I've been benching the players but it's doing no good."

"I think maybe it's the coach who has a case of the yips," she says. "Bench yourself until the end of the half."

"Thanks, coach," I say. "I'm going to try it."

After I click off, I have a rim of wondering faces looking at me.

"I'm sucking this up," I say. "Al will coach for the rest of the half." And I sit down.

"Hah?" Al says. But then he rises to the challenge. "Alright ladies, just like we did it in practice. The up step first. Watch my hand for the variations."

The up step? Oh, that was Wordback for the step up, find the hot player. Trouble is, we have no hot players.

"Izzy, lookie there!" says Al, pointing into the stands. Some crazy fan is holding up a sign. *"Where's Izzy?"* it says, referring to a famous sign in a Guns n' Roses video. I'd been looking the wrong way for a sign.

"Izzy is the git url for the up step, everybody clear?" Al says to the team. Git url? Oh, it girl. It isn't so crazy, right? The starters all nod and head back out into the fray.

Sweet gets the ball and goes up for a shot, but instead of shooting passes to Isabella. Isabella does her hot butter knife trick. And one! Back to sixteen deficit.

"Okay!" says Al, shouting out the play. "The gun and run!" The run and gun is well suited to Isabella's style, good call! And we get hot. But the Seawolves stay hot, and run and gun right along with us. Izzy gets 10 points in the second half of the first half, but we're still down 15 at the buzzer. But we've stemmed the tide.

"I'm back in," I tell the team at halftime. "And Gracie will start the second half. Vanessa C., sit next to me and tell me who's hot and who's not. And Al, great job."

"Fuckem," he agreed.

At first it seems I haven't found the groove. Gracie gets fouled hard and misses both free throws. Stick with it, I tell myself.

The Sea Wolves huddle. Gracie takes a pass and they deck her again. Yikes. But this time she gets up, dusts herself off, and drops them both. Our fans haven't had much to cheer for tonight. Now they stand up and start to howl, land wolves on the trail of sea wolves.

Don't piss off Graciela Jones! The vibe turns and she's all over the barn. She scores, she passes to Iz and Sweet, she's pulling down offensive rebounds and getting another 30 seconds. And the crowd hasn't sat down since she sank the free throws. The Sea Wolves' lead is diminishing.

Give them credit. They don't crack and fold. They play with heart and fire. It is a thrilling game. Gracie seems to have grown a couple of inches. And I can still see that glow around her. But she isn't standing in front of the lights any more.

A pass out to Gracie at the three point line. She rises and the defender hits her, a stupid foul. Gracie isn't a very good three shooter. But this one goes in. And one! Next time down, she gets the ball and gets slammed to the floor. The crowd starts to roar. They know what's coming. We can all feel it.

Gracie sinks the first free throw. The game is tied. The other coach substitutes to slow it down and hope Gracie rattles. The Diametrics see their chance and take it. They stand up without their instruments and start to sing. And soon everyone in the hall is singing along. It is too loud to play basketball in. The ref holds time still out.

I find myself singing along. Graciela is wrung with emotion, and holds her hands in front of her face, while Sweet pats her back. The Sea Wolves can't rattle her, but we can.

Amazing grace, how sweet the sound,
That saved a wretch like me.
I once was lost, but now I'm found,
Was blind, but now I see.

Later on I watched the video of that scene being replayed on ESPN during our next game with Maryland. Venice got the drama of it down well, commenting, "Graciela Jones is a senior who hasn't played as much as she would have liked, who hasn't been an impact player as she would have liked. But for these 20 minutes she has carried the Metrics and played her career game, the game of her life, and the fans are making up for lost time. They have fallen in love with their Amazing Grace. And here if she can compose herself, she will put the Metrics into the lead for the first time since the first minute of the game."

The barn now quiets down. The ref gives Gracie the ball. Bounce, bounce and up. Nothing but net.

There are three minutes left to go. When we're up by five, I take Gracie out so the crowd can salute her again. Twenty points in one half! Everybody should have a day like this. Bring on the lovely Monroe Victory Song! Bring on the lovely Amerie's tune! War to the Feck! Maybe there's a halo around me!

After Marvin's latest story comes out, called "At the Edge of Disaster with the Metrics," I had 250 e-mails waiting for me. It took me an hour to go through them. Some of them actually credited me for the win, rather than Marvin. The most important one was an e-mail from the Provost. It was an invitation for me and the team to come to tea with the Provost and Mrs. Provost Don the afternoon of the Maryland game in the Provost Assembly Room of the Castle, Monroe's Admin building. These invites were few and far between and a sign we were making waves.

As I was finishing the e-mails there was a knock on the wall (remember, my cubby had no door) and there was Marvin himself, looking a little ragged.

"Shakespeare!" I greeted him. "I've been reading your fan mail. Some of them are calling you Marvelous Marvin! Where'd you get the halo part from?" I said. "You didn't interview me."

"I talked to Al Romero," Marvin said. "Turns out he can say more than just 'fuckem.' "

"Well, it was true enough," I said. "I just didn't remember talking about it to Al."

"Coach pillow talk," he said.

"Actually, that would be Dee for me, not me and Al," I said. "But I take your point."

"Coach, I'm here to ask your advice," Marvin said. "From your previous career as a journalist."

"Oh, well, let me try to think back that far," I said.

"This Metrics series has been great, but it's getting out of hand," he said. "There's even a few Marvin groupies."

"You're a young guy, that should be an answer to a dream," I said.

"The series is going around the country now," he said. "The Aggregator Syndicate. One thousand websites. Coach, I'm not even a real staff member at *The Rattler*. I don't have time to go over there to the Snake Pit."

"Well," I said, "either you're a genius or a lucky schmuck. If you are a genius, this is the beginning of your marvelous career, and I salute you. If you're a schmuck, enjoy this while you can."

"I've been hired by *Sports Illustrated* to do a freelance piece on the team," he said.

What? Marvin was eighteen years old and he'd landed a gig some sports journalists never got. Me, they'd hired me to do a book review of Henry Aaron's autobio. Just that one piece in 25 years of sportswriting.

"Well, congratulations," I said.

"I don't know if I can do it," he said.

"Sure you can," I said. "Just do what you're doing in the Metrics series. Don't get the writer yips. You have all access to the team except the locker room. And even there, Karla can take you back if the ladies are dressed." I had a thought. "And here," I said, handing him the printout of the Provost's invite. "Come along to the tea," I said. "Maybe you'll get some color."

"Yeah, I'll need all the angles I can get," he said.

"How about an interview with the coach-on-leave?" I said. "I'm only keeping the chair warm for her, you know."

"Dee? Sure," he said.

"How about the Diametrics?" I said. "Talk about color. I can put in the good word for you."

"I know Stan and Henry pretty well now," Marvin said. "But I'll take you up on Dee."

"Let me call her now," I said, grabbing the cell. "Dee? How about marrying me for better or for worse and for lunch? And can I bring an and-one?"

I never got the bad dreams in the afternoon. So after we messily polished off the ribs and mac I'd stopped to pick up (my pregnancy cravings again), and drank the iced tea, I retreated to my favorite chair for a nap, leaving interviewer and interviewee one-on-one in the study.

A minute later it was a considerable time later and Dee was smiling above me, with Marvin behind her.

"Hum," I said. "Did you get what you need, Marvin?"

"I think I can get something started," he said.

"Dee, we got time for a game of checkers?"

"You'd better get back to practice," she said. "You've got Maryland to get ready for."

"You going to do a third basketball memoir, coach?" Marvin asked.

"I think I will," I said. "I'm going to call it *My Wife and the Beautiful Game*."

Dee laughed. "Pele won't like that," she said.

"He won't kick," I said. Dee sighed and rolled her lovely eyes.

"Who's Pele?" Marvin said.

"Come on," I said. "I'll tell you on the way back."

I was pondering the Maryland team as I drove back to the Zone after dropping Marvin off on campus. (I guess he went to a class or two every once in a while.) The Terrapins, or Terps, were our biggest challenge to date. They were eighth in the country and averaged 80 points a game. We'd never scored as much as 80 points in a game this year.

I never called the Terps the Twerps. That was juvenile. I had too much respect for them. But I figured the Pins was a legitimate shortening of their name. So it was the Pins I was worrying about. How to play them?

There was an e-mail waiting for me when I got back. It was from the Scorpion. I laughed to see it because I hadn't thought about it. But it was good news. I went out to the arena.

"What are you running them on, Al?" I asked him.

"The three 'Fro," he said.

"Good, that fits what I want to do. After I have a chat with them, I want you to drill them on the dicky sea fence. We've got to hold the Pins' scoring down."

"The ladies are pretty good at the dicky sea," Al said. "I'm going to enjoy this."

"Give them a hit on the whistle," I said. "Why don't I have a whistle?"

"Have to requisition one from the Scorpion," Al said. He blew high and sharp on the whistle. "I'm having a couple of beers with him tonight, I'll ask him," he said. "Bring it in," he shouted, and the ladies trotted in from where they were lined up for free throws.

"We're going to have to slow the Pins down," I said, "so Al is going to drill you on defense today. I want the Pins to be breathing in your shampoo. *Claro*?"

"*Si*," said Carmen.

"Alright," I said. "On another matter, I have a note from the AD. We've been evicted from the Zone."

Protest and confusion from the team. "Never did like those Kulls," said a voice. "Uck-fay oo-yay to them."

"You got it wrong," said another voice. "That Pig Latin. In our language, it would be yuck foo."

"Yuck foo young," said another wit.

"Listen now. So two days after the Maryland game, we've got to pack out, clear the lockers and everything," I said.

"Why?" said Sweet. "Bane in the putt."

"Well," I said. "We're going on the road to Providence and Boston College. And when we get back, we'll be lockering somewhere else."

"Where that?" a voice said.

"The John Littlejohn Recreation Center. We can move in if we want, get used to the facility before we open it against the Dames."

"The Wreck," said one of the ladies, comprehending. "The new Wreck."

"Unless you'd like to stay here with the clogging bathrooms and cold water running in the showers," I said.

The team didn't take long to decide. Movin' out of the stanky Zone! Movin' into the newest cathedral of women's basketball.

"Time in," I said. "Al, resume."

I was watching practice idly a few moments later when there was a loud BANG and I looked up. A couple of Metrics were on the deck. Fighting! I ran over to separate them. It was Lara and Vanessa C.

"She got to call me by the initial," Vanessa C said. There was blood coming out of her nose.

"No blood on the floor," I said, repeating a cardinal rule of women's basketball. "Vanessa C, go over and see Karla. And you, Lara, what were you thinking of? How are we going to beat the Pins if you two can't play together?"

"Sorry, coach," said Lara. I was going to do something but I saw Sweet's nostrils flare. Nuff said. "Resume," I said.

I walked over to where Karla was stuffing Vanessa C's nose. "Get ready for another patient," I said.

Sure enough, about two minutes later there was another BANG. Lara had somehow acquainted herself with the deck. Now blood was coming from HER nose.

"No blood on the floor," I told her. "Go over and see Karla. And then I want you to sit next to Vanessa C like you were best friends. I want you two to talk to each other about how we're going to beat the Pins."

Sweet came trotting by, accidentally I suppose. "Nice work, cap," I said to her.

"The Lord works in mysterious ways," she said.

That Friday afternoon was Dee's final outside appearance before the hospital. She told me so. She wanted the chance to drink tea out of porcelain cups at one of Lavina O'Malley's *soirees*.

"We got time for checkers, Dee?" I asked.

"Come on," she said. "Another time."

I'd never been in the Provost's reception room before. It was furnished to the period of the Castle itself, meaning about 150 years old. Nice! The Ivy League schools could stuff it. We had our own traditions in New Netherlands. You ain't much if you ain't Dutch!

The photo op that appeared on *The Rattler's* website later that day was funny. The whole team, doubtless to Lavina's horror, were holding their teacups on their heads.

A couple of courtesy jolts of tea along with the Freak Paeans were dispatched in the company of several dozen bigwigs who applauded us when we came in through the high doors. Then, the Provost had an announcement that would liven up our genteel crew.

"Too small in here," he said. "Let's adjourn to the Multi-Purpose Room." The MPR was a long, light-filled room with a small stage and piano.

And when we did, there was a surprise awaiting. There were the Diametrics, band and cheer squad, instruments and uniforms—well, half of them. True to form, they weren't wearing any skirts or pants. Crazy bastards! They were all wearing royal blue Metrics shorts and playing the Monroe Victory Song.

It dawned on me why a couple of moments later when the Diametrics burst into song. What a thunderous pounding! And I knew the song, I knew the song—

"Of course!" I said to Dee. "It's '1 Thing!' "

What a colossal arrangement they'd made of the old go go rhythm! It must have taken them two weeks. The sharp percussive barks of the horns scraping the Bam-pause, Bam-pause-pause of the drums. The hip swirls of the cheer squad. Their shorts mimicking the short-shorts Amerie wore in the celebrated video.

The Metrics broke into their own dance, hopping into the hip hop with their easy physical grace, their unfeigned exuberance, their ownership dance on the top of the globe. I felt like dancing too, but in loyalty to Dee who couldn't, I didn't either.

And then to top it off, in true Diametrics style, when the song was over they put their instruments down, turned smartly around, and gave us a chant I thought had been retired.

"We got class! We got sass! We got a real Raggedy Ass!"

And then they all dropped trou with the royal blue shorts, showing rows of smileys. The Diametrics Moon! I'd seen it rise many a time, and let me tell you, it's an honor just to be there. Lavina turned and retreated in a huff, but Provost Don had a quiet grin.

"How can we lose tonight?" he said to the assembled crowd. "Let's peat the bins!"

"That's my cue," Dee said. "I want to get off my feet. Can you get me a ride home?"

"I'll take you home myself," I said. "And I'm going to beat you at checkers this time."

Whoever thinks climate change is bogus is out of their minds. It was the middle of February and it had warmed up so the snow had all melted and there was fog all over everywhere in New Netherlands. But the forecast said we were going to go back into the Siberian deep freeze for the big game. Oh well. You make your own warmth in basketball and hope to avoid having to hike across the snow like the good doctor.

The Pins were ranked number eight in the country. My plan to stop them was to step on their sneakers so they couldn't get those threes. Anybody could foul out except for Isabella and Caroline Sweet.

"We're going to run the dicky stee," I said to the team, assembled in the weight room. "I want you to put rocks in their pockets. Don't worry about foul trouble. That's why we have eleven players. (Actually ten with Earlene out.) We defend any shot from midcourt in."

I paused. "I want you to know I'm proud of you. We've won five straight. We're more than half way to the Wreck. The pundits say it's all beginner's luck, I'm making this all up as we go along. But you're not. You're a great team that gelling right now. I've seen the great Metrics teams, 2012, 2013, 2015. This team is going to be remembered in that company."

"Coach, we still under .500," said a voice.

"Check again the end of the season," I said. "Now, the Pins are doing so well because of one dominating player."

"Anaconda," said a voice.

"Correct," I said. Anna Kandel was a woman mountain, big and strong and fast. "So we have to tire her out. We're going to run the three forward on her the first half. Then we go back to our starting five and Star. You give Anaconda the big squeeze."

"Free thorward," Al Romero amplified.

The Diametrics are playing "1 Thing" as we come out of the tunnel to applause and whistles. "No dropping trou," I say to Stan and Henry as I wave at them.

"I don't know," Stan says to me as I go past. "We *are* on ESPN tonight."

Al Romero is looking nervously at the Diametrics. "Are they going to throw the moon tonight?" he asks me.

"Do chefs go to Asshole School?" is my reply.

I look up at the media booth. It's full tonight. There's Marvin. The Metrics are back! And there's Brad in the AV room, with his arms up. Play the song? I draw my finger across my throat. Ix-nay!

Here comes Venice and her producer. Tonight they are interviewing *me* first.

"Nick Johnson," says Venice, admiringly. "Your 1 Things are the talk of the town. You've won five straight, knocking off two top-twenty teams in convincing style. Now you've got a top-ten team to play. Will the streak continue?"

"The Terps are a tough team and Anaconda is one of the premier players in the league," I say. "We've got our work cut out for us."

"What are your chances of making the post season?" she says.

"I'm taking the regular season first," I say. "The rest will work itself out."

"Well, you've got the hot hand and a gym full of noisy people," Venice says. "Good luck coach. Have a gate graham."

Lara, Vanessa C and DNA run the game on Anaconda. They're running at her on offense and double- and triple-teaming her on defense. It is the dicky stee, to be sure.

On offense, it is Lara and Vanessa C who baffle the big girl, dishing off or shooting, wherever the percentage is better. Anaconda grows tentative, and now she's throwing off her whole team. Our sticky dee is holding down their scoring to record lows.

"What's the word, Al?" I ask. This time he surprises me.

"Needles and pins," he says. A joke!

The bright lights say we are winning by 5. Lara gets called for her third foul, and then her fourth when I don't sit her down right away. Tradition says sit her but I'm not planning on playing her in the second half. In she stays.

The move immediately pays off. Whip pass to Vanessa C. Two! Whip pass from Vanessa C. *And one!* Three! A three pointer! With a minute left. When Anaconda tries to barrel past her, Lara sets herself up for the charge but doesn't get the call. She has fouled out in the first half! But I don't mind.

"Great work, Lara," I tell her as she trots in to the bona fide applause of the crowd. "Star, do your thing." We are up by eight at halftime.

ESPN has asked to interview me with Lara and Vanessa C. Between the two of them they have 24 points and

12 assists. The baffled Maryland squad has 22, their lowest-scoring half in history, I find out later.

"We're here with the stars of the first-half effort by the Metrics," says Venice, holding the mike. "Lara Antipova and Vanessa Blaylock."

"C," Lara interjects.

"What?" says Venice.

"Vanessa C. Blaylock," Lara says.

Venice takes the correction. "Vanessa C. Blaylock," she says. "You two have baffled Anaconda and run the offense while the Terps keyed on Sweet and Isabella Matie. But Nick, Lara has fouled out in the first half. I haven't seen that happen in a long time. What now?"

"We've got ten players on the team," I say.

It's odd how your stars can become your secret weapons. But each half of a basketball game has its own energy. Starbucks goes in and promptly blocks a jumper by Anaconda. Swat! The crowd roars. They are starting to smell it.

Our guards? Oh yes, Izzy and Caroline Sweet. Our stars. This is *their* half. The shots start to go down for our guards, and the air is draining out of the Pins' balloon. We have a chance to hold the Pins to their lowest-scoring game in history, but I'm playing to win, not to humiliate them. With four minutes left and us up by 16, I put in the rest of the Beeline. Amazing Graciela gets a big hand when she reports in. I put in Carmen and Roshanti and Sula to give them some playing time. Don't want any of the starters to roll an ankle or worse.

I see something that impresses me. We don't hold the Pins to their worst game ever. They top that by two. But the Beeline plays them even. When the buzzer sounds, we are still up by 16.

Are the Diametrics happy we've won our sixth straight? Boy howdy. They are throwing their instruments up in the air and catching them before coming down to play the Monroe Victory Song for the sixth time in a row. Is the crowd happy we've played our last game in the Zone and soon will christen the new Wreck? Boy howdy. They come piling out onto the court.

But it is Sula who gives me my biggest present of the day. As I'm in my cubby, listening to the ladies cavort and shout in the locker area, Sula comes in holding a copy of a letter.

"Forgot to give this to you before, coach," she says, and then skips happily back down the hall. I open it. It is a Wells reversal letter. Ursula is in good academic standing, still in line to earn a degree and still eligible to continue to play for the Metrics.

It is Marvin's *Illustrated* story that makes us nationwide news. "The Metrics' System." As always he has everything, even the Wells letter and reversal, the Diametrics dropping trou in front of the Provost's wife, the ice cream cavorting ("Diary of a Dairy Run" is how he put it). And he even had a sidebar on me, with my peregrinations from reporter to poetry coach to head coach. So *that's* what he was talking about with Dee as I napped!

I got more than a thousand e-mails when the article came out. Most of them were great but some of them were a little nuts. I got a few marriage offers, a few Craigslist offers, a few job offers, a few odd requests, one of which had to do with endangered squirrels (I kid you not). I was invited to come to Uganda to meet the general's wife, she really does exist and all it takes to meet her is a 50K buy-in. Maybe after the season!

Metrics Fever started to take hold in the patriotic streets of New Netherlands. Royal blue *Go Metrics!* signs started showing up in shop windows in Sheridan City and bunting with our colors (royal blue and white) was put up in official buildings and of course, all the campuses. "1 Thing" was on heavy rotation on the college station, and I was amused, driving to work through a sweet soft snow, to hear Stan and Henry talk in an interview about the crazy shit they were planning if we went to the regionals or nationals.

Just now we were still a sub-.500 team even with six straight wins so it was premature to think about March Madness just yet. February Madness was quite enough for me, thank you.

Dee was braving the discomfort of late pregnancy far better than I ever could have. She'd been to the doctor and he'd said two weeks was his best guess, though the window was two weeks before the due date to two weeks after. If the baby didn't come by then, they would induce labor. We made plans on how to get her to the hospital if I was away.

"King me," I said to Dee three days after the big beat of Maryland. I wasn't going to win, but at least I'd gotten a checker to the end row and earned a supersizing.

Dee had scolded me before about not getting out earlier for our road trip. The bus was leaving at 3 PM. We had two away games in a row, against Providence and Boston College, and our bus coach, soon to be named the 1 Thing by the ladies, would be waiting.

"We have plenty of time," I said. We were going to be away two nights so I had to take advantage of my home time.

I just liked how warm our little house was, a warmth that came not just from a thermostat but from Dee and the life she was carrying. Outside the Siberian Express was running, but inside the home fires were burning.

"You can be my King," she said, and took my hand and kissed it. Must have been those hormones again. Hormones or no, nothing stopped her from beating me. But I wasn't playing to win against Dee. I was playing to be in her life.

"It's so sweet you want to stay with me instead of your hareem," she said, when I was finally ready to go. "That's how I know you love me. So I'm not jealous of how you love your other women."

"Okay, well, you get any twinges or anything you call me," I said. Then I was out into the palace of the wind. The Third River was freezing over again, and the winds coming off it were no nonsense.

The bus was waiting for us not at the Zone, where we'd cleared out our stuff the day before, but at the Wreck. When we got back from the road trip the Scorpion had promised us that we could move in and start practicing there. The building looked quite finished from the outside but of course work was still going on inside and would for a couple of months until all the loose ends were tied.

"Our future home, ladies," I said as I took my seat in the bus. "Back on Monroe home ground, sacred home ground," I said, as my women nodded and smiled. Or were already lost in their headphones. "Eddie, let's drive," I said.

Now when the movie comes out this will be the montage part. (And there will be one. Remember, directors, Johnny Depp for me and Kerry Washington for Dee. Dee and Miss Washington, sorry about the size of the part. The role of coach's wife in a movie usually sucks. But we'll have a few things out of the ordinary. Like the checkers games!). A whole slew of cell phone photos. There's the team and I in front of the 1 Thing bus with Eddie and Marvin. Happy happy joy joy! There's Al Romero, giving his bus spiel about the great state of New Netherlands. And now rolling, rolling, rolling, counting the cars on the New Jersey Turnpike, and then a shot of us getting off the bus late in the night in Providence, tired tired and miserable, miserable. Here we are the next day sightseeing Providence in the 1 Thing, the river there is lit up with fires that rise up out of the water and the girls are gasping with delight. Here's Sweet, leading us all in prayer. Here's

Roshanti rising up for a three that night against the Friars, she gets five of them after coming in for Star who has a rolled ankle, and we win our seventh game in a row. Here we are in the hotel, a toilet paper fight, don't ask, and playing strip poker with the Diametrics, they lose, then us grumpy grumpy rousted out of warm beds to drive up to Boston to play the Eagles. Rolling, rolling, rolling again! Here's one of the teacher and the class in front of the museum on the field trip. Oops, sorry, that's from *To Sir, with Love*. Here's a photo of us at BC, the "Hail Mary" fullcourt pass from Vanessa C to Izzy, who goes up to win at the buzzer, a great game all the way through. There are the ladies whipsawing their bodies around in a circle dance, ready to hear the Monroe Victory Song for the eighth time straight. Now rolling rolling rolling down the turnpikes again, and in another couple of days rolling rolling rolling to Washington to play the Hoyas of Georgetown.

Stop the movie! We don't take the 1 Thing to our nation's capital after all. I'm in my office, this one with a door, at the new Wreck when the Scorpion comes in and allows as how we might be able to scrape together enough money to charter a flight. Oh, doctor, we are back in the big time!

I remember that DVD alone of all of us checked a bag, which earned her a new nickname and earned us a delay at the airport while we waited.

"DVDiva! What's in the bag, gold bricks or something?" says Sweet, annoyed.

"Just a few things I need," DVD says. "Now where is the…" she pauses. "The claimage blame."

"The what?" says Vanessa C.

DVD tries again. "The baggage claggage."

We all cracked up. The baggage claggage! Of course!

"You know what?" says Isabella. "This Wordback is wordwack. Let's say what we mean, and mean what we say."

We can still take a couple of photos with our wristwatch cameras, though. Here we all are in the National

Cathedral in DC, as our captain, Sweet, kneels and asks the Savior for strength and grace in battle that night. We are all Church Ladies for that hour. Here's one of Al Romero dancing the 1 Thing that night as the Diametrics go to (George)town on it. After all, it was DC moves, this was a go go homecoming. That made us the *de facto* home team, and the home team has the advantage, isn't it so? And here's one of me throwing my notebook in the air after we handily beat the Hoyas in our new home town.

On the short flight home, all of a sudden I'm an authority. "Coach," says Izzy, "why the houses in Georgetown so narrow?" (Something about taxes.) "Coach," says DNA, "one of the toilets in the Wreck floods when you flush it." (A call to facilities ought to fix that. What am I, the plumber?) "Coach," says Sweet, "how are we going to beat the Dames?"

Her question brings me up short. I've been concentrating on the ride, not the destination. The ride was a very improbable nine game winning streak which has brought us to respectability, above .500 at 16-15. But now we were going to have to beat Notre Dame, the number 3 team in the country, in front of a national TV audience, with a full gym of Monroe supporters expecting and demanding the first win in our new house.

"Well," I say to Sweet, "we have to stop the Mosquito."

The Mosquito is Louisa Musqueda, the Dames' star senior. She is the heir to the great Notre Dame stars, Venice Sanchez, Skylar Diggins, and the legendary duo of Blue Sky and Blue Waters, and has been playing like a superstar all year long. Tall and tough and quick, she is hard to slow down and her sting is fierce. I think she's a cousin of that Musqueda-Lewis that played for UConn a couple of years ago.

"Piece of cake," Sweet says. "I'll pray on it."

Thanks, Sweet. We're going to need it.

We did have another bus ride, a rock star bus the Scorpion commissioned to take us home from the airport at Arkadelphia. Bunks and all. The ladies wasted no time in sacking out. Marvin sat by me.

"Ready for the big game?"

"Ready as I'll ever be," he said. "Win against ND and I might get another article in *Illustrated*." His grand early success had changed Marvin. Now, instead of thinking he was sixteen, I would have said seventeen.

I had a text message from the Scorpion. *"Snackaround on I. Stop at KBZ."*

"Alright, sleeping beauties," I said as Eddie pulled the bus into the Wreck parking lot. "The AD is buying your snackaround tonight, in recognition of a superior team. He already called it in to the Kaboose, so we should be able just to pick it up. Who's coming with me?"

Sleepy athlete grumbling.

"Al, you're with me," I said. "I need another volunteer. Sweet, you're the captain, you're volunteering."

The cold and new snowshowers had discouraged any welcoming reception for us in the parking lot. We hustled over to the Kaboose across the street. There was a new decoration right inside the door, a suit of armor with a cigar sticking out of his gob.

"Picking up for the Metrics," I said to the guy behind the bar. "The Scorpion called it in."

"Don't know nuthin about it," he said. "Try the Pool Room."

Annoying, this! But I sent Sweet ahead to scout. She came back in a minute, emptyhanded.

"Coach, you'd better come see this," Sweet said.

My patience was wearing thin as I came into the big billiards room and saw a sign:

WELCOME HOME METRICS. BEAT ND!

A loud crash of cheering erupted from kids popping up from behind the pool tables and pouring in from the other rooms. I turned around to Sweet.

"Get the rest of the team in here," I said to her. "Looks like Snackaround is at Kaboose tonight."

"Don't mind a couple of beers," Al said to the clamoring kids. "Who's buying?"

Metrics hoopla was increasing. Local groups were asking me to speak at their lunches. One problem. I wanted to have lunch with my wife. Al Romero, though, had no such standing engagement. I don't think Al paid for lunch once in any of the seven or ten days before the big game that we were home.

I could safely ignore the hundreds of e-mails pouring in, but now my phone was ringing all the time. I turned the volume control down to zero and picked up the phone for about every third one.

Could the team come to Miss Keeler's kindergarten class and meet the future basketball players? Sure, after the game. *Could my daughter play for the team next year?* Well, there was always a walk-on screening, but you had to actually be enrolled at the school. *Could I get them tickets? Right near those kooky Diabolicals?* Tough one, the Wreck opening had been sold out for two weeks.

I was trying to figure out a strategy and I was having trouble. Coaching yips, maybe. But the Dames didn't have any weaknesses. The Mosquito was the best guard in the conference. The Dames were good on defense, good on forcing turnovers, good at three pointers. Well, maybe it would come to me.

One thing I knew for sure. This unusual February was about to end. Our game was Tuesday, Feb. 28. My ten-game contract and the month would go off hand in hand.

I watched Al running the ladies through plays we no longer used Wordback to describe. They looked good. Loose. Rested. They'd had a few days since the Hoyas game and we hadn't been drilling them hard so they'd be good to go for the big game.

"What's the good word, Al?" I said to him. "We're ready to do this thing, right?"

"Fuckem," he agreed.

I am back in the Wreck. The old Wreck. And the building is on fire. As usual, there is only so far I can go in before I hit an invisible wall I can't get through. Daria will have to get to me. I can see her running. *Make it this time!* The damned fireball is exploding, she's not going to make it. She is close to me this time, so close. I see her face as the conflagration reaches her. It is calm, serene. I shut my eyes, I can't watch this. But then I open my eyes and the fireball is gone. Daria is standing in front of me. *She's okay!* I feel her take my outstretched hand through the invisible barrier and she gives it a squeeze. I try to yank her through to safety, but she shakes her head. She is smiling now. I can see her lips move. She is saying something to me, but I can't hear her. She smiles again, and then she starts to recede. *Don't go! Don't die!* I say. But Daria fades farther, and then fades away.

"I'm not going anywhere," says a voice. I look around. I am crying in bed. Dee is looking at me, concerned, not ready to touch me until I am out of dreamworld. When I am, she hugs me. "I'm not going anywhere," she repeats.

I get up to sit in the chair while Dee goes back to sleep. Something outside the window catches my eye. It is snowing.

I must have dozed because next thing is I hear my phone go off. I get up to answer it and it's Mookie, my agent.

"*Bubelah*, you're all over the media," he says. "Congratulations."

"Thanks for the good wishes, Mookie," I say. "I have to get ready for the game."

"You're playing today?" Mookie says. "I thought it was once a week like football. But listen, I just got the lists for today and Sunday. Your book. It's number 8 on Amazon Kindle. And you're number 22 on the *Times* best seller list. You get on ESPN again and I think you'll get into the top 15."

"What?" I say.

"You remember how you asked me what you could do to promote your book?" he says. "You just keep right on doing this. And hey, you talked about new books the last time we talked. What was it? A combined first book and second book? Great, let me write a proposal. How about a third book? Everybody loves a trilogy."

This is all hard to comprehend. And I think I'd better file it away until after the big game. I'm still woolgathering in the chair when the phone rings again. It's Mookie again.

"You sitting down?" he says. "I just got off the phone with a producer. He wants to make a bid on your book for a movie. An option. Free money. If they actually do the movie they have to pay us again."

"A movie," I say.

"Yeah, he's all over it," Mookie says. "He says there's an outside shot at Johnny Depp. But if Kerry Washington isn't available for Dee, what would you think about Rosario Dawson?"

Does a Chef Go to Asshole School?

At lunch, Dee looks at me as I feed Spotter some table scraps. I've told her the dream but I'm still feeling low.

"Big game today, coach," she says. "You need to get your head on straight. The ladies will feel you, and it will throw them off."

"Yeah," I say. I'm not convinced.

"You know, this dream was different," she says. "Daria got through the fire, one way or another. She was telling you she was good. She was telling you you don't have to look after her any more. She'll be good from here. I think she was saying goodbye."

I think about that a while, and I start to smile. "Oh. No," I say. "She wasn't saying goodbye. She was saying *Beat the Dames*."

"Now, it's time to be off," she says. "You'll have to do interviews with the media that's going to be there."

"Not until we play checkers," I say. "I think I see the way to beat you."

"Well if it's that way, then set up the board and give it your best shot," Dee says.

And in fact my strategy is working and I'm ahead of her. I have four kings and I'm zooming all over the board.

"You have a strategy for checkers," Dee says. "How about for the Dames?"

"It'll come to me," I say. Dee is trying to distract me from the checkers, but I'm not going to fall for it.

"You know, with this snow, they may be delayed getting out of South Beach," she says, meaning South Bend (you are supposed to think about the difference between the two). "They might be tired and out of sorts."

I'm looking at my kings and seeing how I can flash them all over the board. Wait a minute! F. Scott Fitzgerald said the hallmark of a first-rate mind is the ability to hold two opposing ideas at the same time. And that's what I was doing now.

Suddenly, my kings zooming around the board aren't male anymore. They are young women in baggy shorts, their startling hair combed back and tied on the top of their heads. I have my strategy. And the other idea is that though I don't bet any more, I am still superstitious. I'd played checkers with my wife before just about all the games we'd won, and I'd lost to her every time. What am I thinking about, winning this time? It is time to tank it.

"You have an interesting mind," Dee says to me as I leave to drive through the snow. "You'll have to tell me about this some time."

I pause at the door. "I do know what Daria said," I say. "I could read her lips."

"What was it?" Dee says.

"Poetry Man," I say.

"Yes," Dee says. "You're my poetry man too."

I have a stop to make on the way to the arena. I had an e-mail from Marvelous Marvin, asking me to stop by the Snakepit to see him. It wasn't far out of the way, an easy park and then a dash past the statue of the Earl of Sheridan, though what the disco earl had to do with Monroe, I had never been sure. The Pit was above the commons, and you could see the statue from the window of Marvin's office.

Yes, office. The *Rattler's* receptionist sighed when I told him I was here to see Marvin.

"Take a ticket," he said.

Luckily, Marvin had been keeping an eye out for me and I got buzzed back. I walked past a couple of dozing reporters (it's good to know not everything in journalism has changed).

Marvin waved me in to an office that said Associate Editor on the door. Its décor could best be described as eclectic, ranging from a framed photo of Jackie Robinson stealing home to a full sized replica of the Venus de Milo.

"Impressive for a month's work," I said.

"Especially considering I'm not officially on the staff," he said. "I haven't had time to fill out the activities card."

I had to laugh. "What's up?" I said. "Kind of a big day for me."

"Kinda wanted to thank you, for the advice and the all-access and all. I couldn't have made such a big splash without it."

"*De nada*," I said. "What are you working on now? Need an interview?"

"No," he said. "I'm working on my pre-game story for the aggregator site. I'm doing it in the form of a dialogue between me and the Earl of Sheridan down there."

"Marvin, I like the way your mind works," I said. "Though I wouldn't talk to statues too much. At least not in public."

"Whatever works," he said. "Did I tell you *Illustrated* has hired me to cover March Madness? Both ends, men's and women's. Anything I want to do."

"That's great, Marvin," I said, getting up to leave. "You remember when we met I said you were either a genius or a schmuck?"

"Yeah. Which is it, coach?" he said.

I smiled and reached over to shake his hand. "I salute you at the beginning of a great career," I said.

I have a visitor on game day. It is Priscilla Barnes.

"You sure saw the opening and took the step," she says after we hug. "Nine straight. And look at this place! The new Wreck. The light bulbs even work!"

"We're having trouble with the hot and cold water, though," I say. "You've done well for yourself too."

"I can admit to you I miss this place, sometimes," she says. "The old Wreck, I mean."

"You'll always be a part of our history," I say. "Your photo is up in the Hall of Fame! Now, you'd better stay with the Dames because Dee's got 40 years of coaching in her here and she's going to win 1,000 games," I say. "But playing the Dames will always be a highlight."

"The Dames," she says, smiling. "We have a mocky name for you, too, did you know?"

"No," I said. "It's a badge of honor. What do you call us? Not the Bitches and Hos? Never liked that one. The Lady Tats? That was okay. Nappy-Headed Hos, no way."

"The Pet Tricks," she says.

"Well, it does rhymes with Metrics," I say. "Fair enough."

"How's Dee?" she asks. "You tell her I love her, 'cause I do."

"Her only problem is keeping me on the straight and narrow," I say.

"You are a little crazy," Priscilla agrees, "but in the most pleasant way. Those backwards words you use! Exacerbating!"

"The whack-ward birds," I agree.

We have our team meeting in the exercise room. Everybody's looking at me. The teammates. Al Romero. Karla Riddick. I'm supposed to talk.

"Okay," I say. "The media is saying *yadda yadda yadda* streaky team gets lucky, rookie coach steps in shit. Now me, I've been checking the bottom of my shoes ever since I got this gig. *(A little laughter from the voice.)* But you guys are the real deal. After tonight you will be part of the storied tradition we have here at Monroe. You'll be the linchpin for this grand new arena we are going to play in, to continue the legends that got started in the old Wreck. They're going to count you in the greatest teams that ever played here and the greatest players, Pip Pippin and Lady Dagger, Horse and House. And after we beat the Dames, no one will question our standing again. You can be proud of what you've done so far, ladies, and Monroe is proud of you. Now, our strategy for tonight. But first, I need to know so I'm going to ask you. Who's going to have the game of her life tonight, because that's who I'm going to play?"

Ten hands shoot up. Eleven, including Karla. Then Karla hears something and suddenly ducks into the corridor.

"Good," I say. "You're all going to play. I want a double team on the Mosquito. Isabella, but I also want a forward on her to give her a hard time. Vanessa C. That's you. And on offense, I want the run and gun. I want them to get run out of this house. Every one of you goes flat out, and when you get tired, I'm sitting you down for a rest. Everyone gets to play."

I am just about done when there's an interruption. Karla comes back in, leading a man who is familiar to me but out of place. Then I recognize him.

"Dr. DeMoto," I say. "Didn't know you were a Metrics fan. Thanks for your support." Dr. DeMoto headed the rehab clinic where I had regained my sobriety. "But you can't be in here. We're having a team meeting."

"Thought I'd bring along a team member," he says, and then I see her behind him. The Goat. Earlene Manigault. She's walking on a cane (what would these stories be if someone didn't walk on a cane?) so it takes her a minute to get in to us.

The players pause for a moment. Then, they erupt into applause.

"How are you?" I ask Earlene.

"Put me in, coach," the Goat says to me. "I'm ready to play."

"Whole team here now, coach," says the voice.

"Well," I say to Earlene, moved. "You know, we never did deactivate you. So if it's okay with Dr. DeMoto, you can sit next to me on the bench."

"Only if I can sit right behind her," Dr. DeMoto said. "This was all a plot to get me a good seat."

"You got it, Doc," I say. The Scorpion could make it happen.

"Thank you ladies," the Goat says. "I want to be a part of this team, now and in the postseason when I get out of rehab. Until then I've persuaded Dr. DeMoto to unblock ESPN on our TV. I want to thank Coach and Vanessa C and Dr. DeMoto, obviously. But also I want to thank those of you who called and texted and e-mailed me. They piled them all up and let me read them."

"We missed you, Goat," says the voice, I believe possibly not being sarcastic for the first time ever.

"Can't play, obviously," Goat says, "but I want to contribute something. I remember two years ago, when coach was our poetry coach. And the championship teams had P.C., the first poetry coach. So there always be poetry around our great teams. Well, I had a lot of time to myself, so I wrote my first poem ever. It's about us, the team." Earlene took a folded sheet of paper out of her pants pocket. "You want to hear that?"

"Absolutely," I say.

"Alright," Earlene says. "It still needs work, but here it is."

We are the Metrics from Monroe.
Wind us up and watch us go!
We're from the New Netherlands,
We have the fastest feet and hands.
We even speak in our own tongue,
So glisten ghostly if you come.
We love our country and our God,
For Beast and Finals we'll get a nod.
But most of all we love our squad.
We love us like we're sisters, brothers,
We'd take a bullet for each other.
We're lovers and *fighters, love our neighbor.*
Except when we pelt them with toilet paper.
It's love that speeds our hands and feet
And makes our shots and passes sweet.
Because with love there's no defeat.
So treat us with the best respect,
When you come and lose inside our Wreck.

There is silence. Then the team moves forward and surrounds the Goat, hugging her, stroking her hair, and speaking to her softly. There are a few tears.

"That does it for here," I say. "Karla, can you post this wonderful poem online and tack the paper up to the bulletin board so we can see it? And ladies, let's go out and christen this sacred house we play in."

Bright lights, big city! The Wreck is full when we walk out of the tunnel and the roaring starts right up. The Diametrics are in their 1 Thing shorts and start pounding out the song. "No dropping trou!" I say again to Stan and Henry. Well, there's no reining in those guys anyway.

Earlene is recognized (after all, she scored one of the most famous goals in Monroe history two years ago) and applauded, till she has to wedge herself upright with her cane and turn and wave to the crowd.

Only one court is available for shootaround because they are maneuvering a stage into the other court for the pregame ceremony. I hear there will be halftime entertainment from the Diametrics, so the stage won't be wheeled far away after the ceremony.

Oh, my morning blues are gone. The moodswings of college basketball can be sharp and a little scary sometimes, but being on the upswing is the part I enjoy the most. I feel a glow around me, and the players, and the Diametrics, and the fans. There is a lot of love in the air. Earlene got it right. We are lovers AND fighters.

The Scorpion has a suit and tie on, there's a first, and he's trying to drag me onto the stage, where I can already see the Governor and the Provost. Just at that moment Venice finds me.

"Coach, it feels like the NCAA finals in here," she says. "And yet it's only a regular season game. Are you confident of winning against a brilliant Fighting Irish squad?"

"Very confident," I say.

"Who's next then?" she asks.

"Well, UConn and Constitution are number one and number two," I point out.

"Have to get past number three first," she says. "Good luck, coach. They want you on the podium."

Damn! Couldn't get away from it.

But wow, here was a different perspective for me, the view from the playing floor. Wow, the fans are close! And their energy is washing all over me.

The Scorpion is standing next to me. "I'll introduce the governor and the provost," he says. "You introduce our special guest."

The governor and the provost were mercifully brief. Then there was the dedication ceremony. The Scorpion said, "We're going to make a special presentation to our team captain in honor of our team and all the great teams that have gone before us. Here she is now, Caroline Sweet."

Applause for our great captain! But she isn't bounding up the stairs as she usually would. Instead, she is shepherding Earlene Manigault and her cane up the stairs.

"Sweet, we'd like you to accept this official basketball designated with today's opening teams and date on it to mark the official opening of our wonderful arena."

Sweet takes the inscribed ball and looks at it. "Thank you," she says. "But I'm going to let someone else hold this ball for the game. That's Earlene Manigault. She's the best basketball player I've ever seen. I can't wait until next year and I wish we could be seniors together. But first, we're going to take care of business tonight."

More roaring! But then there's applause for someone else, and it must be me. Scorpion has just introduced me.

"Thank you," I say. "I've been around the Metrics and the Wreck for many years, both inside and outside the program. This is an inspired program, and I have been fortunate enough to meet and admire some of the finest people there are, your student athletes of the Monroe Metrics." *Applause at this!* "This team, and the other teams I've met, are wonderful representatives of this great university, the great city of Sheridan City, and the great state of New Netherlands," I say. "The Monroe community has existed for centuries now, and I'm sure it will exist for centuries more. This team will be remembered for what they've done and what they still will do. Our spirit, and the other teams' spirits, will live here for as long as that is." More applause.

"But I'm forgetting what I'm up here to do. You know, we call this basketball palace the Wreck. But really it is called the John Littlejohn Recreation Center. And I'd like to introduce our founding spirit, our greatest coach, and one of the greatest of all time. He won 800 games and is even prouder of the hundreds of athletes who have left Monroe with academic degrees. I give you, John Littlejohn!"

Littlejohn comes bounding out of the tunnel. But when he gets to the podium, he chokes up after saying "thank you" for the waves and waves of applause by the fans. He shakes his head, accepts his dedication trophy, waves it to the crowd, and steps down from the podium.

Provost Don says "I now declare the John Littlejohn Recreation Center to be officially open."

Let's play ball!

"What's the word, Al?" I ask Romero.

"Fuckem twice," he says. "And listen, I got something for you for luck, for the big game."

And he hands me a beautiful thing, a bear's tooth necklace with braided horsehair for a chain.

"This is gorgeous, Al," I say. "Where did you—"

"My grandmother," he says. "She was Native American."

I put the beautiful thing on for the game. "Thank you," I say. "And I want to thank you for the great help you've been to me. I'll tell the Scorpion about it."

"Fuckem," he agrees.

Something catches my eye on the court, where the players are lining up for the tip.

"Look at that!" I say to Al. "Izzy's got her arm up!"

"It's for the tip," he explains to me patiently, as if to a six-year-old, as Denzel might say.

"But it's her bad arm," I say. "She's all healed."

"World watch out," Al says.

We mean business from the get go. Starbucks rises in the air to control the tip to Sweet, and she's down to the hoop in a second, with the Mosquito trying to flag her down. *Up two!* On the next possession, Isabella steals the ball and beats everybody down the court. *Up four!*

We're not known for the run and gun so the Dames are confused. They look flat at the outset. Sweet and Vanessa C. sandwich the Mosquito on her first shot, and I think Star might have gotten a small piece of the ball. The ball disappears in a scrum, and DVD comes up with it. Now she tries scooting back to the goal, but she's not as fast as our guards and it's one on three. You can see she's going to the bucket anyway, but at the last minute the ball goes backwards, to Vanessa C., and she rises for the three. *Up by seven!*

The Dames are too fine a team to crack. They furiously try to compensate for the Mosquito's lost mojo. They try threes. They try the lanes. They chase my players like there's a hurricane at their tail.

My ladies are playing balls-to-the-wall (well, you know what I mean). Sweet is hot, and Isabella is finding her everywhere except the bathroom. Starbucks has decided she is going to get every rebound. DVD gets free twice and sinks threes.

At the third media timeout we're up by 12 but my players are flagging. "Lara, I'm keeping Vanessa C in. But you and the Beeline are going in. Keep it going for us."

My intuition about the Beeline comes in big. The Dames start to click. With Sweet off her, the Mosquito starts to get untracked. But the Beeline is also playing as if it's their career game. It is a score-a-thon back and forth, exciting basketball on both ends. No one is going to the free throw line. No one can lay a hand on each other.

Here comes the Mosquito downcourt with her eyes on the prize. Lara is racing behind her, and when the Mosquito goes up for the shot she sticks her long slender arm in there and—*smack*! Denied!

When I take the Beeline out with three minutes to go in the half, the place erupts. They have played the Dames dead even. We're still up by 12.

Sweet two! Isabella three. Mosquito three! I swing my arm to keep the pressure on. I hate slowing the pace of the game down to protect a lead. You just throw your own team down. Run and gun! And the Dames are running and gunning against us.

When the buzzer sounds, we are up by eight and we have 50 points. One of the Scorpion's employees runs down to me and says, "That's a record half for the Metrics! We've never scored 50 before!"

Venice finds me and Sweet for a quick interview but I don't have to talk. I smell the virtuous sweat on Sweet, and it is a beautiful fragrance. Venice says, "Caroline Sweet, you have 20 points in the half and your 1 Things are exploding all over the gymnasium. What's your secret?'

"What's our secret? Well, I told you I'd tell you some time. Here's what it is. Here's the one thing we know. This poem from the Goat laid it all out for us. It's devotion. We live for love and devotion. For the team, for the fans, for the school, for the game. We the warriors of love and devotion and God is love, so we His most virtuous daughters."

"Well," says Venice, "an unusual take on what has been a most unusual game so far. Back to you, Trey, for the halftime show."

They are wheeling the stage out again and bolting it down. The Diametrics in their shorts are surrounding it, but the stage will never be able to hold them all. My ladies aren't even going back to the locker room. The halftime show is the worst-kept secret in the history of the university.

The lights dim for thirty seconds, and when they come back up somebody is on the stage. She is wearing a glittery tuxedo jacket with frilly shirt and bowtie, and a pair of

Metrics' royal blue shorts. But they look a lot better on her than they do on Stan and Henry.

"Sheridan City!" she says. She points to the team in front of her. "My *playas!* My crazyass band! When I heard what you all were doing with my song I had to come down here and work it with my Diametrics. It's called '1 Thing!' "

Sorry for not explaining that it wasn't Emory that had called me that day. It was Amerie. When I passed her over to the Scorpion they'd hatched up this wonderful plot, which had been leaked to the *Rattler* by special runner to the Snake Pit and the radio station as if it was a Super Bowl commercial.

With the Diametrics cutting up the rhythm and Amerie singing, and the team gyrating around, I start to think I have seen everything.

When "1 Thing" is over to great applause, Amerie comes to the mike and says, "We don't have much time but I got a new song I'm going to do for my *playas*. Light it up, Stan and Henry!"

The Diametrics bang into another go go beat, and Amerie starts to sing the "oh, ohs." She sure did write this for us! It's called "Rebound!"

I'll be your rebound,
You catch me and pull me down...

I don't have a good defense,
I don't mean to take offense,
I'm just waiting for the sound
That says you'll be my rebound.

Oh, oh, oh, oh,
Oh, oh, oh, oh.

Baby, I know the score.
You're mine, I want to be yours

I will take what I have found
And get you on the rebound.

After she finishes, the Diametrics put their instruments down and drop trou. I'm getting to know these Raggedy Asses a little too well. But the capper is, Amerie on stage mimes dropping her shorts as well. Imagine that going viral! But she doesn't, and bows instead. *Applause for Amerie!* A talented and sexy woman.

The Scorpion's man is back again. He says, "We've never scored 100 points in a game. Ever. Push for it if you can."

"Tell the Scorpion I'm looking to win," I say. "I want the score to be us up by at least one at the buzzer."

But nothing is going to cramp my high this night. Not only does everything have that glow around it, I can't feel my feet any more. I'm kind of drifting around not touching the ground.

The ladies are buzzing from the Amerie concert. We huddle briefly, my only chance to brief them on the half. "Samo," I say. "Starters in."

The Dames are totally back on their game. They're playing the run and gun, trying to narrow it down. Even a big lead can be erased if the other side cracks. But we aren't going to crack. Sweet, for three! Izzy with her hot knife going through the butter to score. Starbucks getting the offensive reebs and the second chance. Score! DVD clearing the defensive boards. Vanessa C getting hot with a couple of threes. Four blocks by Lara, my big Ukie volleyball sixth man.

But the cumulative effects are starting to tell on my starters. They are tired. It's early, but I put the Beeline in. They are fresher. They are fresher than the Dames, too. Roshanti gets the rebound. Outlet pass to Lara. Bounce pass to Carmen. And one! Sula steals and finds Amazing Graciela, who scores.

Time out, Dames! The hall is starting to sing "Amazing Grace" but the Diametrics strike up something else and it dissolves into general mayhem.

This shift the Beeline actually outscores the Dames by two. I sit them down and put the starters back in. Don't want them to rest too long and get stale. We're up by 14.

Those Dames. They crank it up a notch and start chipping away at the lead. The Mosquito starts to sting us. We can't seem to stop her. We just need Izzy to find Sweet and give us two more. Up the floor. Steal, down the floor. Up the floor again. The Dames are turning the run and gun around on us. My ladies are tired. The lead is down to six.

I put the Beeline back in to rest the starters for a few minutes. The lead dips to four, but then Gracie gets a three. The next time down, she gets another three. And the next time down, a third three! We are up by fifteen. Time out, Dames.

Traditional wisdom dictates putting the starters back in. But they're toast. They've all played career games already. Sweet has 32 points. Iz has 15 assists. Starbucks has pulled down 24 rebounds. DVD has six threes. Vanessa C has made eight straight free throws. Lara has five blocks.

The Beeline is back in. And they appreciate the vote of confidence. They take it up a notch. The Dames are game. They run and gun with us. The Mosquito has 36 points. We're up by 12 as the game winds down. I swing my arm. It's against my rules to slow a game down. So Gracie gets her fourth three with just a few seconds left. We have scored 100 points.

The players are shrieking and knocking each other over at center court as everyone in every seat starts surrounding them on the court. The Diametrics get swamped and only a few of them can break into the Monroe Victory Song for the tenth straight time.

Venice with her mike stops me from getting to the players. "Unbelievable, coach," she says. "And we just heard upstairs. Monroe is being seeded twelfth for the Beast. So you're in the postseason after all. Good luck!"

I'm trying to think of something to say to her when the Scorpion's man reaches me for a third message.

"What?" I say. Did I hear him right? The water's broken again in the showers? Don't I have enough to worry about?

OMG. *The water's broken.* "Son, help me get out of here," I say, leaving Venice to cope with the bedlam after our first victory in the new Wreck.

I'm not sure why I got thrown out of my wife's delivery room, but I sure did.

It was at some ridiculous hour. I thought I'd been behaving myself and even being helpful with wet washcloths and the occasional breathing advice (that, by the way, was *very* virtuous sweat!). It had been ages and ages, though by the way we count time it was about 12 hours, I guess. It gets pretty real in maternity. There was screaming in there. Not the three grunts and a six-months-old baby popping out you get on the TV.

Anyway, when push came to shove (I'm talking literally) Dee started pointing at me and saying "I don't want him here," in what I thought was a rather too-loud voice. Vehement, you might say.

The nurse took me by the arm and escorted me out into the neonatal waiting room. "Don't worry," he said to me. "When the wife starts yelling at the husband, he's going to become a father in the next fifteen minutes."

I was alone in there and I was very alone. Why was I so tired? It was Dee doing all the work. I thought about it quite hard, believe me. In fifteen minutes would start the biggest responsibility I would ever have. Was I strong enough? Did I have the stamina?

I spent those fifteen minutes as if I was with somebody else, as if I was rating a potential freshman for next year's team. And I got the clarity I was looking for. I was ready.

So I was smiling already when the nurse came back in fifteen minutes and said, "Coach, you have a beautiful daughter." Of course it was a daughter. With all the female energy around me (even my dog!), how could it be any other way? *Right answer*, I thought. *A beautiful daughter*.

"Can I see them both?" I asked.

"Of course you can," the nurse said.

Dee was holding something in her arms. But my first thought was for her.

"You okay?" I said. "Really now."

"I'm fine," she said.

Okay, this is a little embarrassing to recall, but the next thing I did was lay my head on her shoulder and start to cry.

"My other baby," Dee said. But as I continued to cry, and I got a little worked up over it, I felt Dee's hand ruffle my hair to sooth me. She had a scent of very virtuous sweat indeed.

"Nick," she said. "I've got somebody I want you to meet." I looked up.

Oh! Oh, I know you already, I thought at this beautiful little being. *I've known you all this time you've been swimming around your mother's belly. You've swum to me from so far away. From Ireland, like my mother. And the Netherlands, like my grandfather. And from Africa, our deepest home. From so far away.*

"Look at these rings of hair!" I said. "So perfect!"

My daughter was looking at me, or looking in my direction, anyway, with a calm, unfocused curiosity.

Welcome to the world, I thought at her. *You're going to need my help, at first. And I'm going to need yours, at the last. Is it a deal, then? Can the Scorpion draw up the papers?*

"Look at her little fingers," Dee said, and I joined my hand over hers and the baby's. And the universe wasn't so big and cold any more. It was only as big as the space our three hands shared. It was about the size of a basketball.

I don't remember leaving the room again but I did. The evidence was I was waking up from a sleep in one of the hard plastic chairs in the waiting room. The nurse had opened the door and stuck his head in.

"Your family is here," he said.

And they were. My Tall Women came in, one at a time, slowly and shyly as wet swans, as Yeats might have said. Caroline Sweet, so tiny in comparison. Isabella Matie, fast as the lightning. Starbucks, powerful and gentle. DVDiva and her "baggage claggage," something I think about every time I'm in an airport. Vanessa C. Blaylock, and don't forget the C. Lara Antipova, from the Ukie dominions. Amazing Graciela, a torch of fire inside her. Carmen. Sula, the queen of the spreadsheets. Roshanti, who's now in law school. They were all amazing, not just Gracie. And they still had that glow around them I'd seen the night before. My 1 Things.

"Sorry I had to bolt," I apologized. "I so wanted to be with you. But I needed to be here even more."

"That's aight. Everybody told us to say hi," Sweet said. "I mean *everybody*. Coach Al, Coach Priscilla, Karla, the Scorpion. Provost Don. Stan and Henry from the Diametrics. Even Amerie, she wanted to hang with her *playas* in the Squat after the deal. Girl can *dance*."

"Don't forget the audio guy," said Isabella.

"Brad, yes," said Sweet. "And Marvelous Marvin. Brad gave me this strange message to give you," Sweet said. "He said, 'Ask him if a chef goes to Asshole School.' "

I smiled at that. "He surely does. He does go to Asshole School," I said. "That's what you say when someone asks you if this hasn't been the most perfect day. Now look…"

"We know," Sweet said. "We get a day off, and then we start to practice for the Beast. We drew St. John's, and they gonna want payback."

"We want to see Dee and the baby if they're awake," said Isabella. "But we have one more person wants to say hello. I'm not going to tell you who it is, but let's just say it's a person of extreme poetry." She handed me a cell phone, and my Metrics all trooped out into the hall again.

"Julia!" I said.

"I'm hearing good things, Papi," said a familiar voice. "I'm hearing everybody's well except you, you a little green around the gills. But you'll get over it."

"She's beautiful," I said. "I wish you could see her. Where you calling from?"

"Just a minute, just a minute," she said. "I'm getting a text, with an attachment. I'm in San Antonio. We're home for three games. I don't mind. Warmer here than where you are. Here it is. O-M-G. A little doll!"

"You got a picture that fast?" I marveled.

"Remember which century we're in, Nick," she said.

"Oh boy," I said. "I can't remember anything, and I can't forget anything."

"I'll be her auntie, what do you say?" Julia said. "I'll show her how to front some really fine poetry."

"Of course, you can," I said.

"And you beat the Dames? And won ten straight? Did you step in shit or something?"

"I surely did," I said.

"What a beauty," Dags said. "Makes me think about when me and Spo-kan Man will be ready."

"You'll get there," I said. "You'll get anywhere you want to go. I'm proud of you, Julia."

"Yeah," she said, fronting some emotion I could feel right through the phone. "Yeah, we're going there. Oh man, time do go by, doesn't it? Remember when we first met? I was all sharp elbows and cuss words, what a brat. What did you ever see in me? And now I'm somebody's aunt."

"You were smart. You loved to talk," I said. "Best source I ever had. And look at you now, a star."

"Yeah," she said. "And look at you too, Papi. It's quite a thing, isn't it? This game we play, this thing of ours, it's about life, isn't it? It's about being alive, and don't get cheated."

"Don't get cheated," I agreed.

"Got to book," she said. "Tell Dee I'll call her, all my ladies probably wore her out."

Something struck me. "I've got to book too. Something important I have to tell Dee. And Julia? I see you on TV. You still have those sharp elbows."

"And I see you a father and I'm keeping you from it," she said. "Go on. We'll talk again."

The Tall Women and my daughter were gone from Dee's room by the time I got there. I was kind of glad. I wanted her alone.

"I'm so sorry," she started, but I waved her throwing me out aside.

"I've got it. I've got it!"

"What have you got besides the conniption fits?" Dee said.

"The name. It just came into my head. Danitra Juliette Johnson." Danitra was my wife's name. Juliette was my mother's name. Johnson was my name.

"Danitra Juliette Johnson," Dee said, trying it out. She thought for a moment. "DJ for short. I like it. That's her name."

"Let me write this down, I said, looking through my pockets for a piece of paper. "How long was she? And how heavy?"

“Six pounds two ounces,” Dee said. “Twenty inches long. She’s going to be tall.”

Neither of us was willing to say it. Instead, I asked, “What was the time of birth?”

“Nine-oh-two,” she said.

“9:02, February 28, 2017,” I wrote down.

“Not quite,” she said. “It was February 28 when you got here. It was March 1 when she was born.

March. *Of course*!

Johnny Depp has a crush on my daughter. To see this most famous of actors clowning around with his scissorhands props to make DJ laugh and shriek is quite a thing for this humble son of New Netherlands to see. Of course, the blades are safe, actually as dull as can be, though Johnny is threatening to make a sequel called *Running with Edward Scissorhands*, so be forewarned. He lives in fear of being called a *jujubee* by DJ. She doesn’t like the candy, so it’s not a compliment to be called one.

Rosario Dawson is a real sweetheart. She’s outrageously pretty (though not quite as tall in real life as you might think from the screen). She laughs all the time, and yet is dead serious about her community and social work. For the second movie (actually from the first book) she reminded me that she turned down *Men in Black 4* to do this film, so I ought to feel special. At my suggestion they used some of the college-aged girls from the Girls Club of New York, a favorite charity of hers, to play some of the athletes, and that’s why she came back.

If you think I’ve gone Hollywood, I haven’t. We spent a couple of weeks there two years ago for the first movie (second book) and a couple of weeks this summer for the prequel or sequel. That’s it. Had to see at least a little of it. If I’d been the director I’d have stuck more closely to the books. But it was his movie, not mine. I never wrote any skiing scene, for instance, and what intelligent basketball player would risk breaking her leg? But I just kept quiet and cashed the checks.

So, did we go on to win the Beast or the NCAA finals in 2017, the season I'm writing about in this third book? Well, to quote Sweet, maybe I'll tell you one day. It's not really germane to the book proper, which ends with us christening the Wreck and DJ coming into the world ready to be christened on the same snowy night and morning. But we did play in both tourneys, and I'm confident our squad will be well remembered down the years. Right after we finished, the Scorpion went out and got a new car, and that will tell you something!

There have been other seasons, and many more to come, I hope. I was glad to keep Littlejohn's percentage up. Nine of my ten players earned degrees (Amazing Graciela was called away to do missionary work for her church right as the season ended). Sula earned her CPA and is now MY accountant. (We don't spend much time talking about Philosophy.)

Three of them have played in the WNBA. Sweet popped an ACL, unfortunately, and now is going to ministry school. But Izzy and Earlene are still in the league. They are all exceptional people, the whole team is. We shared some precious time together. They are welcome in our home any time. My 1 Things.

The funny thing is, we'd all stopped using Wordback by the time it went viral. So if it annoys you, it's all right to blame us. But it's just a fad. It will pass. Have a date grey!

Will there be more books after this one? Well, never say never. But you might ask why Dickens never wrote another book on Scrooge. His happy life, after he gave over being a miser, got about one sentence from the Chuckster, if I recall right. It just isn't great copy.

Happiness isn't a conspiracy. It is its own thing. It can be our thing, if we're lucky enough to get in with a terrific bunch of people. But it starts very close to home. If the rest of my days are happy and dull, so be it. Be happy for me in my little Dutch Colonial house, in the great state of New Netherlands.

DJ loves to go with me to the Wreck to watch her mother at work. So do I. She is only four but already well versed in the game and the merits of the opponents. She can do a nice little chant on Geno Auriemma's first name, for instance. It rhymes with *mean-o.*

"What do you call that line, Daddy?" she might say, pointing to the semicircular three point line as one of our shooters rises behind it.

"The arc," I'll tell her.

"So our guards are arc-angels, right?"

"I think they must be," I'll agree. She definitely has a little bit of the poetry in her already.

A minute later she is on her feet, protesting the lack of a call. "Come on, ref," she pipes up. "You're missing a good game here." But the two of us, we weren't.

These days it is me that stays home and Dee that goes to work, and now that I'm bringing in enough not to be sponging off her, I'm totally happy with that. I guess I never told you in so many words how much I love Dee, did I? But I'll tell you this. We were able to resume traditional forms of afternoon affection, but the high point of my day is when she comes home for lunch and has time to play checkers with me. I even beat her, every now and then.

I wish I could tell you I have sweet dreams, but the truth is I don't remember them any more. Spotter still patrols my mornings to make sure I get up without ambush.

I'm keeping my fingers crossed, then, that the applecart of my days will not get upset. I take them as they come, and appreciate the little miracle that they do come, that we get a new 30 every time the sun comes up. And I know, that if I ever crave excitement and that rollercoaster of ups and downs, that glorious mountain of elegance and anguish and poetry, I only have to wait for March Madness. It comes every year, to make bearable that dreary month between the ice palace of winter and the flower palace of spring.

LOVERS *AND* FIGHTERS

We are the Metrics from Monroe.
Wind us up and watch us go!
We're from the New Netherlands,
We have the fastest feet and hands.
We even speak in our own tongue,
So glisten ghostly if you come.
We love our country and our God,
For Beast and Finals we'll get a nod.
But most of all we love our squad.
We love us like we're sisters, brothers,
We'd take a bullet for each other.
We're lovers *and* fighters, love our neighbor.
Except when we pelt them with toilet paper.
It's love that speeds our hands and feet
And makes our shots and passes sweet.
Because with love there's no defeat.
So treat us with the best respect,
When you come and lose inside our Wreck.

REBOUND

Oh oh, oh oh oh
Oh oh, oh oh oh

I'll be your rebound,
You catch me and pull me down.
As I go with you up the floor,
I love you more and more.

I don't have a good defense,
I don't mean to take offense,
I'm just listening to the sound
That says you're my rebound.

Baby I know the score.
You're mine, I want to be yours.
And then I'll take what I have found—
I'll get you on the rebound.

Oh oh, oh oh oh
Oh oh, oh oh oh

You don't have to be tall to play.
You'll know it when you feel this way.
I'm telling you I'll stand my ground
When I ask you to be my rebound.

About the Author

MARK FOGARTY is a writer, journalist and musician who is the author of seven books of fiction, three of poetry (*Myshkin's Blues*, *Peninsula* and *Phantom Engineer*), a nonfiction book on rock and roll and a book of Christmas stories and poems, *Christmas Cheer.* He is a graduate of Rutgers University and the editor of the New York City trade publication *National Mortgage News*. He has had many stories and poems published in literary magazines around the country. *All That's Best of Winter Light* is the third volume in a series, a valentine to the players and coaches of women's collegiate basketball, a sport he has followed for many years. He also has written a trilogy of books of fiction on rock and roll (*The Sheridan City Trilogy*) as well as a trilogy of pulp fiction (*Annals of the Reborn*). His fan's notes/memoir on rock and roll, *Went to See the Gypsy*, is now in its second edition.

www.ingramcontent.com/pod-product-compliance
Ingram Content Group UK Ltd.
Pitfield, Milton Keynes, MK11 3LW, UK
UKHW020128250726
13967UKWH00002B/543

9 781300 727057